W.J. Corbett w   the People
were living orde   hen humans
appeared. But s   People soon
had cause to hic   . Sometimes
by chance the   le met and
legends were b   mutual fear
and suspicion.

So began the   ear between
the large and th   mischievous
magic were wh   esides of the
humans. In tu   their young
ones to flee the   d destroyed
with thoughtle   or countless
generations th   mans lived
uneasily together, each avoiding the other.

The *Ark of the People* sequence contains stories
of the Willow Clan taken from their history books
– their loves and laughter and their courageous
battles.'

Born in Warwickshire, W.J. Corbett joined the
Merchant Navy as a galley-boy when he was
sixteen and saw the world. His first book, *The Song
of Pentecost*, won the prestigious Whitbread Award.

'Mr Corbett has wit, originality and economy
with words which put him straight in the very top
class of all   f such classics as
*The Wind   h, *Daily
Mail*

THE SPELL TO SAVE THE GOLDEN SNAKE

W·J·CORBETT

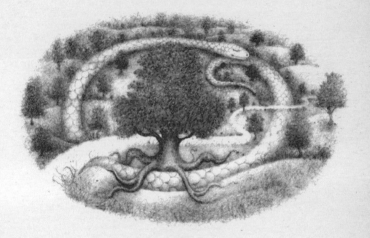

Illustrated by Wayne Anderson

Hodder
Children's
Books

A division of Hodder Headline Limited

To Sophie, Rachel, and Cerys Morbey

Copyright © 2002 W.J. Corbett
Illustrations copyright © 2002 Wayne Anderson

First published in Great Britain in 2002
by Hodder Children's Books

The right of W.J. Corbett to be identified as the Author
of the Work and the right of Wayne Anderson to be
identified as the Illustrator of the Work has been
asserted by them in accordance with the
Copyright, Designs and Patents Act 1988.

10 9 8 7 6 5 4 3 2 1

A Catalogue record for this book
is available from the British Library

ISBN 0 340 85064 7

Typeset by Avon Dataset Ltd, Bidford-on-Avon, Warks

Printed and bound in Great Britain by
Clays Ltd, St Ives plc

Hodder Children's Books
A Division of Hodder Headline Limited
338 Euston Road
London NW1 3BH

Contents

One

A Boy Called Nettles

Peaceful seasons came and went in the valley of the People. A fresh green spring and a warming summer gave way to a fruitful autumn. Then came the snapping frosts of winter, always a delightful time. And then it was spring again.

A whole year had passed since the band of young adventurers had returned from their quest to find the end of the tail of the Great Golden Snake. Their mission had been a great success – despite a few mishaps. But the folk of the Willow Clan back home in the family oak were forgiving souls – they would always forgive the odd blunder if made with the best of intentions. For who was perfect? All serious quests were bound to meet with problems along the way. So the people of the clan had proudly cheered their loved ones home. It was good to see the youngsters arriving back at the great oak, wiser and filled with learning about life beyond their valley home.

Thanks to the brave questers, the great snake had achieved his long and wept-for desire. His head was at last reunited with his tail, that end of himself that had freakishly grown to become a winding wanderer around the valley of the People for the past one thousand years. Now he was an awesome, golden sight on the hill as he dreamed through the first seasons of his planned one hundred years sleep, his tail tucked comfortably under his chin. In the rays of the sun and the glow of the moon his sleeping body resembled a huge circlet of gold, beauteous beyond compare. He seemed to be quite lifeless, except to the Guardian Clan who knew that his great heart ever gently pulsed.

The guardians of his life now became the guardians of his sleep. Utterly devoted, they continued to tend his needs, scrubbing away the flaking golden skin and offering gifts of fish and honey when he opened his huge jaws to yawn in his deep sleep. At night, around their fires on Buttercup Hill, the elders of the Guardian Clan would tell their infants how, one day, the great snake would awake. How he would ripple with life once again. Then there would be a great festival to celebrate his return to the land of the living. Then the youngsters would witness the smile to top all smiles, as their parents had promised. A smile so wonderful as to make the toes tingle. A beam that would make them fall instantly in love with the Great Golden Snake. Having heard the story many times before, the youngsters would start to yawn. As far as they were concerned, the great snake belonged to history, and should remain there. But the young ones had an even greater boredom; the dragging of heavy stones to plant upright in the earth around the sleeping giant. Why they were forced to do it they had little idea. The elders said they were building a stone circle, a Snakehenge around the body of their sleeping hero, a monument that would immortalize him for ever. The youngsters could see no sense in the idea at all, which made the task more tedious. Why waste precious time dragging stones up the hill, when they would rather be roaming around and playing?

Meanwhile, high in an oak tree down in the valley of the People, another youngster also had the yawning bug. He had been yawning every day throughout the past four seasons, and he was convinced that he had more reason to yawn than anyone else in the valley.

In a kitchen caverned into the home oak, a boy

stood dreaming in a cloud of steam. Beside him was stacked a pile of dirty soup bowls waiting to be scrubbed and rinsed to sparkling freshness. The boy's name was Nettles.

'*Why* must I be a trainee cook?' he muttered to himself. 'My destiny is to be a great warrior, not a stirrer of stews! But Granny Willow will never understand, and all the while my dream is passing me by. Didn't I prove my skill and courage during the quest to the end of the great snake's tail?'

His daydreams were rudely interrupted.

'Nettles,' called Granny Willow across the kitchen, 'when you've finished the washing-up, I've another job for you. And stop daydreaming, there's a good boy.'

'Another shaming job, I suppose,' grumbled Nettles to himself. 'I finish one and there's always another waiting. Will my misery never end?'

'What was that?' asked Granny Willow sharply. 'And be sure to scrub those bowls with lots of elbow grease. I won't have uncleanliness in my kitchen!'

'Yes, Granny Willow . . . no, Granny Willow,' sighed the boy. 'As usual I'll scrub until my fingers are red and raw and wrinkled. Fingers that were born to wield a sword and draw a bow. Oh, the great deeds I could do if given the chance!'

'I'll help you wash the soup bowls, Nettles,' piped an eager voice from a corner of the kitchen. 'I've finished chopping my vegetables.'

'No, thank you,' said Nettles, not even glancing over his shoulder. 'You do your job and I'll do mine. I'll manage quite well, if left alone.'

At this the piping voice began to sniffle and sob.

'Must you always hurt Poppy's feelings?' said angry Granny Willow. 'She's only offering to help, after all. I won't tolerate bullying in my kitchen, my boy. Apologize to Poppy at once, do you hear?'

'If I've hurt your sensitive feelings, I'm sorry,' said sullen Nettles. 'Just stop snivelling, I can't stand girls who weep to get their way.'

'Now ask Poppy to help you with the washing-up,' ordered the lady. 'And smile as you ask her politely.'

'Would you like to help me with the washing-up, Poppy?' snapped the boy over his shoulder, 'as you're dying to poke your nose in my affairs?'

His answer was a squeal of delight. Moments later his adoring admirer was at his side, happily rinsing the bowls as he scrubbed them. The boy ignored her shy smiles and glances. In his own mind he was a warrior, and had nothing in common with a humble kitchen-maid, though he did sneak a look at her through the billowing steam from time to time. He could not help but notice her rosy cheeks, spiky black hair and how her green eyes flashed with adoration whenever he looked her way. This pleased and annoyed him at the same time, for Nettles yearned to be admired as a warrior and not a trainee cook. So he hurried through the washing-up, in the hope that Poppy would scurry back to her corner and leave him alone with his dreams.

'I'll be over to inspect the soup bowls in a moment,' called Granny Willow, sweatily stirring her cauldron of stew, 'to scan them for lingering germs. You know how I feel about germs buzzing around my kitchen.'

'No germ would dare enter *your* kitchen, Granny Willow,' grinned Nettles. 'If it did it wouldn't get out alive!'

Soon the old lady came hobbling over to inspect their work.

'There's a good boy and girl,' she smiled, patting their steamy heads. 'As clean as I'd wash them myself. And now for your next job, Nettles. I've noticed that I'm nearly out of fresh herbs and my secret ingredient, which is most vexing. For a stew is not a stew without my special things to boost it.'

Nettles brightened at once. These days he lived only for his rare trips down to the stream to gather fresh herbs for the kitchen. There he could act out his dreams of being the warrior he knew he was born to be. Hurrying to his private nook in the kitchen, he sorted through his treasured things. Buckling on his sword and slinging his bow and quiver of arrows across his shoulder, he returned to receive Granny Willow's instructions, his nerves tingling with excitement.

'Right, listen carefully,' she said, counting off on her plump fingers the items she needed. 'Lots of wild garlic, of course. Plus plenty of parsley, mint and thyme. But most important of all, I need a sprig of the secret red flower we never name aloud. Whisper that name to me, Nettles, for kitchen walls have ears in this valley of jealous cooks.'

'A sprig from the tiny red sunset flower that hides amongst the brambles,' whispered Nettles into her ear, 'which I must stuff inside my tunic in case I'm being spied upon. And I must not touch the root of the sunset flower because it contains magic best left alone.'

'Stuff the sprig as deep as possible inside your tunic,' urged the lady. 'For a secret ingredient is only secret if it's not known by all and sundry.'

'I know all this, Granny Willow,' said Nettles, impatiently. 'You've sent me down to the stream many times before. I promise that your secret ingredient will be stolen only over my dead body.'

'There's a brave, obedient lad,' said the lady, pleased. 'So young, yet so skilled at keeping my secrets. You'll make a wonderful little cook one day.'

'Also over my slain body,' muttered Nettles to himself. 'A warrior I intend to be, the art of cooking is not for me!'

'So,' said the satisfied lady, 'are you ready to tackle your next vital mission, my brave boy?'

'Ready, Granny Willow,' said the boy, proudly checking his weapons. 'If a rival cook tries to steal my secret herbs I'll run them through with this sword.'

'I'm ready too, Granny Willow,' piped Poppy, emerging from her own private corner of the kitchen.

Nettles gaped. She was no longer the little drudge he had judged her to be. Gone was the drab shift she always wore for her kitchen duties. Now she was dressed in a bright red tunic and a jaunty hat brimmed with feathers. Around her shoulders was draped a purple cloak that added to her sudden mystery and in her belt was tucked a tiny dagger, which she toyed with in a business-like way. In short, she looked every inch what Nettles had despaired of her being. She looked absolutely stunning. And the arrogant boy was clearly stunned as he gazed. But he felt anger too, for pretty as the new Poppy was, she had no right to intrude in his private adventure down at the stream.

'She's not coming with me, Granny Willow,' he said, stubbornly. 'I've always gathered the herbs alone. Poppy would just get in the way if I had to defend them. Why can't she stay here with you? You must have lots of work that she can do. I'm sure that your kitchen needs scrubbing from top to bottom once more.'

Poppy began to sob again, wiping her eyes on her purple cloak.

'You'll take Poppy, or you won't go at all,' said the lady, sharply. 'She's been hinting for ages that she'd love to gather herbs with you. So don't be unkind. Ask the girl to go with you.'

'Have I a choice?' said the bitter boy.

'Not even the glimmer of one,' said Granny Willow, shaking her head. 'So I advise you to ask away.'

'Poppy,' asked Nettles, grudgingly, 'would you like to come herb-gathering with me? But you must promise to do exactly as I say. There'll be no giggling or squealing if we're attacked by giant wasps or envious cooks. A fluttering girl could ruin my mission.'

'I'll be your steely butterfly,' promised delighted Poppy. 'Just happy to flutter in your presence, noble Nettles.'

Once again she flashed her green-eyed gaze and his anger subsided. Her adoration was so total that Nettles was beginning to bask in it. Though only a simple kitchen-maid, her attention was better than being ignored by practically everyone in the Willow Clan. So the ambitious boy accepted her as his first adoring convert, his first disciple on the road to power. He could always discard her as he gathered more important followers, he reasoned. And she did have an attractive way about her, he had noticed *that* from the moment he had first glimpsed her face through the billowing clouds of steam. And who knew, perhaps one day she would measure up to his idea of a perfect partner. But that was for the future to decide. At this moment everything was a question of wait and see.

'Off you both go then,' said Granny Willow, hugging them. 'Remember all the items I've listed, and bring them safely home. And yourselves quite safe, I pray.'

'I'll bring you back a present, Granny Willow,' grinned Nettles. 'While I'm down at the stream I'm going to cut you a strong hobbling stick for your bad legs, to help you hobble more easily.'

'And I'm going to cut you a nice bunch of flowers,' said happy Poppy. 'A sniff of spring for a very nice lady.'

'Away with you both,' scolded a pleased Granny Willow. Then sternly to Nettles – 'And remember, not a word about the secret thing you stuff inside your tunic!'

'If Nettles blurted a word, he'd feel the sharpness of my dagger,' vowed Poppy. 'Even though I admire him a lot.'

'Me, blurt out a secret?' said Nettles, enraged. 'Just remember who's in charge of this mission. I'm only taking you because Granny Willow has forced me to!'

'No arguing!' snapped the old lady. 'You must learn to work together as a team. Your herb-gathering trip will surely fail if you fall out at this early stage. Just keep in mind that the fragrance of my stews depends on you returning home with the vital things I've listed. Now let me see the backs of you . . .' and she shooed them from her kitchen, happily turning back to bustle amongst her pots and pans.

Nettles and Poppy were glad to be out of the stuffy kitchen, eager to begin their adventure in the fresh air of the outside world. Soon they were swarming down through the branches of the giant oak to the grassy floor below. A few early risers were already pottering about, gathering mushrooms for Granny Willow and snipping cuttings from their favourite plants to grow in their tree-gardens high above. Not far away a group of clan warriors were practising their archery and sword-play skills. Nettles felt envious as their captain yelled commands that were instantly obeyed. How he wished that he had such power. He would have lingered to admire them longer, but the early gardeners wanted to gossip – being of the People they were naturally nosy. They stopped digging to ask Nettles and Poppy where they were going so early, and dressed in such warrior finery. Poppy was about to blurt the answer when Nettles nudged her to silence.

'We're bound on a vital mission,' he said, grandly. 'A mission so secret that we can't breathe a word. I can only say that the nourishment of the Willow Clan depends on our success.'

'Sorry we asked,' said the offended gardeners.

'We didn't know that Nettles the kitchen-boy had become so important. We can only say that being pompous suits you, small washer of dishes.'

'But doesn't Poppy look pretty?' remarked someone. 'What a pity she chooses to walk out with scowling Nettles.'

'Nettles looks grim because he has a lot on his mind,' said Poppy, quickly. 'When our mission is over he'll be his grinning self again.'

'Must we stand chattering?' scowled Nettles. 'We need to get down to the stream as soon as possible.'

'Oh, going down to the stream, eh?' said someone. 'What for?'

'I'm not allowed to say,' snapped the boy, hurrying by. 'Our mission and our destination are a secret.'

'But you've just told them our destination, Nettles,' said Poppy, dashing to catch him up. 'I just heard you blurt it out!'

'You hear too much,' warned Nettles, pausing to wag a finger. 'If you insist on twisting everything I say, I'll send you straight home to Granny Willow. Is that clear?'

'Yes, Nettles,' said the girl, obediently. 'From now on I won't hear a thing. You're perfectly right to tell me off, you being so perfect in my humble eyes.'

'I'm not perfect, Poppy,' smiled Nettles, patting her feathered cap. 'Just almost so.'

'Modesty so becomes you, Nettles,' replied Poppy, flashing her beautiful eyes at him. 'What a perfect partner you'll make some lucky girl! Forgive me if I hang on your every perfect word.' And she was determined to do so, even though they passed a blackbird warbling a perfect throatful of notes as they neared the bank of the stream. She also ignored the fact that this was a perfect spring morning with the sun shining just so. And not even the perfect music of water rippling over pebbles could change her mind as they arrived at their goal. None of these perfections could move her heart as she gazed at Nettles, eager to carry out his orders.

'Right,' he said, brusquely. 'You know what wild garlic looks like, and parsley and mint and thyme. So get gathering. And keep your eyes peeled for a truffle or two. Well, what are you waiting for?'

Then rudely turning his back, he plunged into a thicket of brambles, leaving her quite alone. Forlornly Poppy began to gather the items that Granny Willow had listed. There came not a word, not even a pained 'ouch' from her hero inside the bramble bush. She was feeling very neglected as she pottered along, stuffing herbs into the pouch at her waist. As she was crawling about sniffing for truffles, there came the sound of delicately fluttering wings. Looking up, the startled girl saw the tiny bird who had sped in to perch upon a twig above her head. Then began a question and answer session, the little creature asking most of the questions. It was a very cocky jenny wren who seemed to know Poppy's business, whatever her business was . . .

Two

JENNY, BRINGER OF BAD NEWS

'That boy blundering about in the brambles,' began the bird, gesturing with her beak, 'surely he isn't the Nettles who boasts about becoming a great warrior? I've heard a lot about his bragging, and I'm curious to meet him. And your name is?'

'Poppy,' whispered the girl. 'And please keep

your voice down, Nettles hates to be disturbed while on a secret mission.'

'Well, Poppy,' grinned the beady-eyed bird, 'I've had a quick glance at him and he doesn't look much to me. In fact, he looks like the trainee-cook he's said to be. In spite of his bow and arrows and sword, he looks just like an ordinary boy trying to be an extraordinary one.'

'I didn't hear that,' gasped Poppy, horrified. 'Nettles has banned me from hearing too much.'

'And another thing,' said the wren in an even louder voice. 'In spite of his lofty ambitions he's barely taller than me! But never mind. If the boy is made of the right stuff, then I'll help him to become a great warrior.'

'Nettles would love that,' said delighted Poppy. Then puzzled – 'But how could you help him to become great, tiny Jenny?'

'Because of what I saw while flying upstream at the crack of dawn,' replied the bird in a grave voice. 'I witnessed a sight that will make you Willow folk tremble. I fear that the People are going to need a valiant warrior in the days that lie ahead. So when will your hero be coming out of those brambles to discuss the terrible situation? Being an expert spotter of worthy warriors, I need to run my beady eye over him.'

Just then Nettles came crashing from the brambles, rubbing his scratches and tucking something deep inside his tunic.

'I heard voices,' he said, suspiciously, 'and talking about me.'

'Not *my* voice, Nettles,' said Poppy, quickly. 'I've only been whispering. The loud voice you heard was Jenny's. She won't go away until she's talked to you in person.'

'So here is Nettles in the flesh,' sighed Jenny, shaking her tiny head. 'All I see is a trainee-cook overburdened with deadly weapons. So where's your cooking pot, ambitious boy?'

'I don't own a cooking pot,' replied the angry boy. 'And I only pretend to be a trainee-cook to disguise my undercover warrior work!'

'Oh, on secret business are we?' mocked Jenny.

'And how many secrets do you know? Not as many as me, I'll bet.'

'I wouldn't tell you anyway,' retorted the boy. 'The point of secrets is to keep them secret. And my secrets are no business of a cheeky wren who should be out gathering moss to build a nest. Also, frankly you're too tiny to bother talking to!'

'You're not so big yourself,' snapped Jenny, annoyed. 'To be brutal you're much too puny to become the great warrior your family will need in the days ahead. A real warrior should tower head and shoulders above everyone.'

'One day Nettles will tower with courage,' said loyal Poppy. 'Quite soon the force of his personality will make itself felt. In fact, his strength of purpose overwhelmed me when our eyes met across the kitchen, as he scrubbed the stew bowls with his strong hands.'

Nettles preened to hear her words. Now he was glad he had allowed her to play a small role in his mission in life, for Poppy made him feel good while asking for nothing in return. In short, she was the ideal companion for his boundless ego, and she was also very pretty, which helped a lot.

'Well, I quite agree with you, Poppy,' grinned Jenny. 'After gazing into his deep brown eyes I'm beginning to fall in love with Nettles myself, even though hero-worship is something new to me. I hope I don't disgrace myself by swooning from this twig.'

'And I hope that you're not making fun of me,' warned Nettles. 'Because if you are, I'll be forced to draw my sword and end this conversation right now!'

'What, make fun of my very first hero?' mocked Jenny. 'Strike me dead if I should do such a thing.'

Hearing this, Nettles calmed down, for he was glad he had not been forced to snuff out her tiny life. Then a thought occurred to him.

'Why have you taken an interest in me?' he asked. 'Why perch for so long on that twig just to take the measure of me?'

'Because I've decided to become your companion for life,' grinned the bird. 'I believe that I can mould you from a common kitchen-boy to a mighty warrior, a hero whose name will echo down the ages when your story is written in the history books.'

'Excuse me, Jenny,' said angry Poppy. 'But I'm going to be Nettles' companion for life!'

'We'll share him then,' said Jenny, generously. 'I'm sure he has room for both of us in his heart.'

'What if I don't want you in my life?' snapped Nettles. 'I think you should wait until I invite you into it.'

'Why waste precious time?' was the cocky reply. 'For as I said, I gather secrets too. And I've a secret that you Willow folk have no inkling of, a secret that could destroy this beautiful valley if not dealt with in time. For a threat to your way of life is approaching even as we speak, a threat that will require a brave leader to step forward and nip it in the bud before it's too late. And I've decided that you are that leader, lowly kitchen-boy. I feel that you are the one who can save this valley and your people from the mortal danger that looms.'

'What danger?' cried Nettles, grasping the hilt of his sword. 'Point it out, Jenny wren, and I'll tackle it right now! Tell me what you know, and quickly!'

'Well, it all began at first light this morning,' explained the bird. 'Feeling the need to stretch my wings, I took a flight downstream to where the waters flow into the sea. Then, while resting on a twig, I saw something that almost made me lose my balance, so shocked was I.'

'What sight almost made you lose your twig-balance?' asked mystified Poppy.

'From a distance it looked like a giant water-skater,' said Jenny. 'But when I flew closer, I saw that it was a huge bristling ship.'

'A ship in our stream?' said puzzled Nettles. 'And bristling with what?'

The tiny bird shuddered. 'Bristling with rows of oars and gleaming axes, brandished by drunken warriors from some northern land, every one of them cursing and threatening to wreak havoc and murder the moment they wade ashore!

And judging by the course of their ship they're heading upstream and straight for this valley!'

'So you took a close look at these strangers,' said Nettles, nervously. 'And were they of the People? Did they look like Poppy and me?'

'They did a bit,' nodded Jenny. 'The same silly snub noses and about the same size. But much fiercer than you. Not the type to tangle with, I'm thinking.'

'What dreadful sailors they sound,' shivered Poppy. 'I always thought that seafarers were jolly folk with their sea songs and jigs. Let's hope that they get shipwrecked before they reach our valley.'

'When do you think they'll arrive here, Jenny?' asked anxious Nettles.

'Well,' the bird considered. 'They're very strong and lusty rowers, so I'd say they'll be dropping anchor at this very spot some time tomorrow. Around sunset at the very latest.'

'Then there's no time to lose!' shouted Nettles. 'I must hurry back to the oak to tell my Willow

Clan about this terrible news. And then I've lots of organizing to do to fend off the threat from these invaders!'

'Spoken like a born leader,' giggled delighted Jenny. 'I knew I'd backed a winner from the moment our gazes locked when you stumbled from the brambles.'

'Don't forget why we came here, Nettles,' reminded Poppy. 'You and I will be severely scolded by Granny Willow if we don't return with her precious herbs. Don't forget we're still bound to her as trainee-cooks. We can't let her down after she's been so kind to us.'

'Granny Willow will get her herbs,' said Nettles, impatiently. 'Then we'll thank her for all she's done for us and hand in our notice. She'll soon realize that our clan needs warriors more than cooks in these dangerous times. The valley must be saved and it looks as if it's down to me.'

'And me,' said Poppy, quickly.

'And me!' said indignant Jenny. 'I'm also a part of the team and a companion for life. After all, it was me who spotted the menacing ship. Don't think you can pick my brains and then cast me aside. You'll be needing me to make more scouting trips downstream, checking on the progress of the bloodthirsty sailors from the north.'

'Actually, our clan has a magpie who scouts for us,' said Nettles, embarrassed. 'He'd be very upset if you put him out of a job.'

'Don't worry about him,' scoffed Jenny. 'I spied him early this morning, lounging in his comfy nest he was, playing with his bright, stolen trinkets. While I was spying out the course of the bristling ship, he was gloating over his ill-gotten gains!'

'If that's true, then Jenny has a serious point,' said Poppy. 'Perhaps our magpie should be persuaded to hand in his notice too. He obviously prefers counting his baubles to being an early-morning scout.'

'Our magpie is the least of our worries at the moment,' said irritated Nettles. 'We'll thrash out his career prospects when we get home to the oak.

Come Poppy, we must make haste to tell our people about the danger that threatens. Do you agree, or would you rather disobey my order?'

'Yes, Nettles,' nodded Poppy, eagerly. 'I mean no, Nettles.'

'I'm also with you, leader mine,' grinned Jenny. 'My heart is yours and my scouting skills are at your command.'

'Come then!' cried the boy. 'Let's race back to the oak with the bad news. And when we get there, I insist that you leave all the talking to me – as your leader, and as a warrior it's only sensible that I should do the explaining.'

'Of course, Nettles,' murmured Poppy as she hurried along behind him. 'Who else but you could possibly be in charge?'

'Who else indeed?' giggled Jenny as she flitted above their heads. 'I've long yearned for someone masterful in my life, and now I've found him. The swaggering boy has made my day, who'd want it any other way?'

Three

Granny Willow Is Not Amused

The folk of the Willow Clan were astonished when Nettles came hurrying back to the oak and ordered them to stop what they were doing. Flushed with excitement he demanded that they gather in the meeting hall at once, saying he had something of vital importance to tell them. The word quickly spread that he was going to give a lecture on some kitchen skill or other, for what else could he know about? Perhaps he had made an amazing discovery that would make washing-up less boring – and that was bound to be boring in itself. But the Willow folk had always been tolerant of anyone who wished to speak in the meeting hall.

'Even kitchen-boys are important,' they agreed. 'After all, we all have to start at the bottom. Perhaps a lecture about washing-up might be more interesting than we think. So long as Nettles doesn't lecture about the art of cooking, which is Granny Willow's special subject. For she knows much more about making stews and baking acorn bread than anyone in the valley.'

'Nettles tends to be over-proud sometimes,' said an oldster, looking worried. 'Let's hope he hasn't launched a revolt in the kitchen and thrown Granny Willow out.'

'We'd never allow that,' said another, firmly. 'A trainee-cook could never improve on the quality of Granny Willow's stews.'

'Let's wait and hear what Nettles has to say,'

they agreed. 'It's only time, after all, and we always make time for the young.'

And so the Willow folk filed dutifully into the meeting hall, determined to give Nettles a fair hearing, for free speech was their pride and they fiercely defended it. Their gossip died away as Nettles and Poppy entered the hall, the Jenny wren fluttering between them. They were greeted by a polite smattering of applause. This was followed by gasps of admiration, for never had they seen Nettles looking so splendid, nor Poppy so pretty. The audience had only ever glimpsed them slaving in the hot kitchen, or staggering into the dining hall with a cauldron of stew, bowls piled high on their heads. While the warriors were impressed by the array of weapons Nettles wore, the ladies were gazing enviously at Poppy's hat, brimmed with freshly-picked primroses. Then Nettles held up his hand and began to speak.

'I won't mince my words,' he cried. 'I've called you here to warn of a disaster that's bearing down on our home valley. A disaster in the shape of a ship bristling with oars and axes!'

'A ship crammed full of rough sailors . . .' shuddered Poppy.

'A ship sailing three parts in the wind because the crew are drunk,' chirped Jenny. 'And to introduce myself, I'm Jenny, the new companion of Nettles. We've agreed that only death will part us.'

Poppy's gaze was dagger-sharp as she smiled and patted Jenny's beak. Then Nettles continued.

'While I was on business down at the stream, I had this strange feeling,' he said, mysteriously. 'As if my whole life was about to change. As if some great hero from the past was urging me to take on the mantle of leadership of our clan. The hero seemed to speak in my ear, saying, "Unsheath your sword, oh Nettles . . . Prepare to defend the valley of the People . . ." '

'No he didn't,' interrupted Jenny. 'The voice you heard was me calling you out from the brambles. Let's get our facts straight, eh?'

'I know you spoke too,' said Nettles, quickly.

'But as I emerged from the brambles, I felt this sudden weight of destiny in my heart. And how right it's turning out to be. But I'll gladly bear the heavy burden placed upon my shoulders.'

'Go easy on the self-glory,' said Jenny, annoyed. 'You knew nothing about the invading ship until *I* warned you about it.'

'Nettles has a sixth sense,' said Poppy, swiftly. 'There isn't much he senses that's worth knowing about. At least, I think that's what I mean. Anyway, I wish I had his gifts, instead of just humbly sharing them as his closest companion for life.'

'When will this cock-and-bull story be over?' yelled someone from the audience. 'Unlikely tales are best enjoyed after meals. And I'm starving for my lunch!'

'I'd like to know who's doing the washing-up!' shouted someone else.

'And who's chopping up the vegetables in the kitchen!' cried another. 'Proud Nettles and pretty Poppy seem to be getting above themselves.'

'Silence!' ordered angry Nettles. 'I'm no longer

the humble trainee-cook of yesterday. I've stepped into the breach to save this leaderless clan and our valley from a shipful of drunken marauders. And all *you* worry about is lunch? You'd better heed my grim warning instead of whining about your rumbling bellies!'

'And you'd better heed my grim warning, my boy!' cried a voice from the back of the hall. Everyone turned to see Granny Willow limping down the aisle, a steaming spoon wagging in her plump fist. She was not amused when some of the youngsters in the hall began to giggle. Pointing the spoon at Nettles and Poppy she spoke on in scolding tones. 'Never mind about this silly craving to be famous,' she snapped. 'Where are the herbs I sent you out to gather?'

'They're safe here, Granny Willow,' assured Poppy, patting the pouch she wore slung over her shoulder.

'And what about the sprig of the tiny red flower whose name cannot be mentioned?' said the lady, glaring at Nettles. 'I hope that your ambition hasn't outgrown the trust we've always shared? And did you remember to leave the magic root of the flower well alone, as I told you?'

'Yes, Granny Willow,' said the boy, hurt. 'And the precious sprig is tucked deep inside my tunic. I'd never let you down, even though I'm going to be famous.'

'Well, you can forget about fame this side of lunchtime,' said the lady, impatiently. 'There's a cauldron of simmering stew in the kitchen waiting to be served. I order you both to step out of the limelight and follow me back to where your true duties lie . . .' and she turned on her heel and made to limp back to her world of pots and pans. But she was stopped in her tracks by two defiant voices.

'I refuse, Granny Willow,' shouted Nettles. 'I'm handing in my notice as of now. I want to be a warrior not a cook, and now my chance has come.'

'I'm also handing in my notice, Granny Willow,' said nervous Poppy. 'My future is at the side of Nettles as his companion for life.'

'So who will chop my vegetables and do my washing-up?' cried the bewildered lady. 'I've only one pair of hands!'

At her words, a forest of hands shot up from the audience. There were many youngsters only too keen to replace Nettles and Poppy in the kitchen, and all just as ambitious too. Seeing a former kitchen-boy and a kitchen-maid standing so proudly and prettily in command, it was obvious that a job with Granny Willow was the first rung on the ladder to fame. Glancing around, the old lady beckoned to a bright-eyed boy and a tiny flushed girl who were waving their hands higher and more frantically than the other hopefuls.

'Very well, I'll take you . . . and you . . .' she sighed, pointing at them with her spoon. Then she turned back to Nettles and Poppy. She was more sad than bitter as she said, 'I've enjoyed our times working together; I hope you have too. I wish you every success in your new careers, whatever they are. Just don't forget me, as I'll never forget you.'

'We won't, Granny Willow,' vowed Nettles.

'We'll come and visit you as often as possible,' promised Poppy, wiping away her tears on the sleeve of her red tunic.

'And now, back to practical matters,' snapped the lady. 'Hand over all the precious herbs to my new trainees. For there's lots of work to be done in my kitchen, with so many mouths to feed. And don't worry about the hobbling stick and the flowers you said you would bring me back. I'm sure you were much too busy to remember.'

Blushing with guilt, Nettles and Poppy handed over their collected herbs. Then Granny Willow limped from the hall, her new helpers skipping happily behind her. Their names were Rosie and Thorn, and they were pleased to become kitchen-slaves if fame lay just around the corner.

Then the conversation returned to the supposed disaster that threatened the valley of the People.

'This bristling ship you speak of,' said Robin, an elder who had been a great leader in his time. 'How do you know that it's sailing in to attack our valley? It could be just a pleasure cruise of happy foreigners enjoying the sights.'

'It might be just a red herring that Jenny has invented,' said Fern, Robin's companion for life. 'Robin and I encountered many red herrings in our adventurous days. And the little wren looks cheeky enough to lay a false trail for her own mysterious reasons. Am I right, little bird?'

'No, you are not,' retorted Jenny. 'I know an angry ship when I see one. Since when did a crew of red herrings swill down beer and swear, and wave sharp axes in the air?'

'What I meant had nothing to do with fishes,' said Fern with dignity.

'Then say what you mean, or say nothing,' snapped Jenny. 'The threat the valley faces is not from silly red fish, but from a shipful of maniacs!'

'Show respect for my family, Jenny,' said angry Nettles. 'Fern is a heroine of our clan, and don't you forget it. I also insist that you leave all the talking to me, as we agreed.'

'Sorry, my leader,' said Jenny, shame-faced. 'I

suppose you and I are having our first quarrel, a moment I've been dreading. From now on I'll keep my beak shut. If you want to be friends again, just nudge me from my grief . . .' and she huddled into a huffy fluff of feathers and pretended to fall fast asleep.

But Nettles was in no mood to pander to her hurt feelings. He had lots of important things to say. He had barely spoken a few words, before there came another commotion from the back of the meeting hall.

'Hello, what's the gathering for?' asked Finn the fisher-boy, striding down the aisle. Close on his heels trotted the faithful Pansy, a basket of shrimps balanced on her head. Like Robin and Fern before them, they were also respected as past heroes. But like all genuine heroes they rarely talked about their past great deeds. In fact, Finn much preferred to talk about fishing . . .

'How's that for a bumper catch,' he grinned as Pansy set down the heavy basket. 'With Granny Willow's cooking skills, we'll all enjoy a shrimp stew tonight. What's the matter, what have I said?'

He had noticed the anxious faces of the folk in the hall, realizing that something was wrong. Then he saw Nettles and Poppy standing on the small dais where usually only important people stood. Though not a snob, Finn was puzzled. How could kitchen helpers rise so high in the world in the short time it had taken him to catch a basket of shrimps? Was such an astonishing thing possible? Then suddenly Nettles was calling down to him.

'Finn,' he asked urgently, 'did you happen to see a foreign ship while out on your fishing trip? A ship filled with fierce warriors, and sailing towards our valley? I ask because you know everything about what glides on, or beneath our stream.'

'Ship . . . I saw no ship,' said Finn, even more puzzled. 'But then Pansy and I were fishing in a quiet backwater this morning. What's going on?'

'You ask what's going on?' cried Nettles, outraged. 'Our valley is about to be invaded and meanwhile you choose to catch shrimps in backwaters? I'm surprised and shocked. I've always looked up to you, Finn, son of Finn of the Fisher Clan.'

'I'm also flabbergasted,' said Poppy. 'While you and Pansy were lazily casting your nets, Nettles was bearing the whole weight of this threatening vessel on his shoulders. The worries on his mind are enormous, though he'd never say so.'

'Finn won't be spoken to like that,' snapped Pansy. 'He's entitled to go fishing if he wants. How can he keep watch for invading ships when he's casting his net for our tasty shrimp supper?'

'Fishing being so relaxing, you see,' said Finn, embarrassed.

'So you've settled for the idle life,' said Nettles, shaking his head. 'Of peaceful back-lagoons and lounging in the sun, while danger rows towards our valley.'

'And Pansy's no better,' said Poppy. 'Paddling in pools with her skirts tucked up and pretending that she's younger than she is.'

'How dare *you*, a lowly kitchen-maid, talk to *me* like that,' said angry Pansy. 'Get back to your kitchen and scrape your vegetables, or whatever you do!'

'An *ex*-kitchen-maid,' said smug Poppy. 'With a tasteful hat-sense that I notice you haven't got!'

'My hat is squashed for a reason,' seethed Pansy. 'It's had to bear the weight of a basket of shrimps. But it's still more fashionable than the gaudy affair on your silly head. If you don't watch your tongue I'll be up there to push that flowered monstrosity over your nose!'

The meeting looked set to end in squabbling and tears. But Nettles and Poppy stood their ground on the speaker's dais, refusing to be budged by the laughter that came from below. It was a brave performance from ones so young. Then, thankfully, a bit of sense entered the hall, in the person of Sage the water-vole heroine. Hearing all the commotion coming from high in the oak she had clambered up the rope-ladder to find out what was going on. More importantly, she had some urgent words of her own to say. After shaking the water from her thick fur over everyone she squelched forward.

Thankful that her friends were merely arguing and not fighting, she began to speak, but to the annoyance of Nettles and Poppy she ignored them and spoke to Finn.

'Finn,' she warned, 'I've just received news about a strange ship rowing up the stream. It appears to be packed with outsiders, all waving weapons and cursing. It's with dread that I fear it's heading towards this valley.'

'Old news,' chirped a scornful voice. Jenny had decided to wake up (if she had ever been asleep at all). 'I delivered those terrible tidings ages ago. And you, plump vole, should know that Nettles is now in charge around here.'

Sage was too bewildered to reply. Before she could find her tongue there came another interruption from the back of the hall. The young magpie had squeezed in through the narrow doorway, his beady eyes filled with worry. He also addressed Finn, not even glancing at fuming Nettles.

'Finn,' he said, shakily. 'As your faithful scout I

have to inform you that danger is steering this way. A foreign ship is approaching our valley, and barely a day's sail away. The occupants bristle with sharp weapons and their war-cries are frightening to hear. I'm sorry to bring such bad news, but as a scout it's my duty to wing it here while it's still fresh.'

'Stale history, you mean,' giggled Jenny. 'Who are you trying to fool? You've been lounging in your nest playing with your bright trinkets all morning, don't deny it. And the one to address your stale news to is Nettles. Finn as a leader is old hat now.'

'Is that true, Finn?' asked the astonished magpie.

'I'm still bewildered too,' said Sage, finding her voice at last. 'Finn, will you please tell us what's going on?'

'I must admit I've been doing a lot of fishing these days,' said Finn, shame-faced. 'But I swear I always remained ready should an emergency occur.'

'Not for this emergency, you didn't,' scolded

45

Jenny. 'Which is why Nettles was forced to take charge of the dangerous situation.'

'Well, I'm here now,' said Finn, annoyed. 'So, know-all bird, when do you think this ship will arrive in our valley?'

Jenny ignored him and spoke to the audience below. 'According to my reckoning the invaders will drop anchor off our valley beach some time tomorrow evening, or perhaps sooner. It all depends on how eager the northern warriors are to cut your throats. It could also depend on how many barrels of strong ale they've drunk. Too much drink can cause even the strongest rowers to zigzag off course. So they could arrive sooner or later than sunset tomorrow. Unfortunately for you, if they arrive later it will mean that they've had too much drink, making them twice as fierce.'

The audience gasped in horror as they imagined a horde of axe-wielding drunkards chopping off heads and laying waste to their peaceful valley.

'Then plans must be made urgently,' cried Finn, all thoughts of fishing forgotten. 'Give me until after our shrimp supper, and I'll have an emergency strategy in place.'

'I'll spring into action much sooner,' shouted Nettles. 'I'll have a strategy in place after we've had our lunch – which is nearly ready!'

'And I'll be planning beside him,' vowed Poppy. 'I'll even skip lunch if Nettles needs me to.'

'And so will I,' said Jenny, her beady eyes sparkling. 'Oh what a trio we will be, just you and him and loyal me.'

'So let the clan decide who will be their new leader,' cried Nettles, searching the faces of the audience. 'Will it be young and vital me, or Finn? Let me be the first to say that Finn was once a great leader of the Willow Clan. But who can deny that he seems to get older and lazier by the day?'

'And why shouldn't he?' shouted an angry voice from the crowd. 'Finn deserves his relaxing fishing hobby after such a noble career.'

The audience applauded and nodded in agreement, though they had to admit that Finn was looking his age these days, and just a bit creaky in the joints compared to the suppleness and the youthful spring in Nettles' step. Perhaps it was indeed the moment to choose a new leader to tackle the dangerous times ahead.

'Let the warriors decide,' said old Robin, sensibly. 'For it is they who will fight the battles to come.'

The Willow Clan warriors in the crowd looked first at Finn the brave fisher-boy, who had led them on the quest to the end of the Great Golden Snake's tail. But now, in sadness, they saw not the bold adventurer he had once been. Instead they saw a shrimp-catcher, and a contented one at that. Then they looked at Nettles. There was no mistaking the lust for battle that burned in his eyes. After a few words between themselves the warriors made their decision, and their spokesman rose to speak.

'The brave Finn will always hold a special place in our hearts,' he said, gazing sadly at the leader he was about to discard. 'But we warriors need a new and dynamic leader to follow into the battle, if we are to save our valley from the barbarians.

So therefore we choose Nettles. We will fight faithfully under his command.'

'And so will we!' yelled the youngsters in the hall. 'Just give us the sharp weapons and we'll do the gory job. Just give us the chance and we'll send the invaders rowing back home with their oars between their legs!'

Finn nodded his head proudly and accepted the verdict. His companion Pansy didn't. She was outraged.

'Don't you ever think that Finn is finished!' she stormed, tears streaming down her cheeks. 'He'll make his comeback, and I'll be there beside him when he does.'

'No, Pansy,' said Finn, gently. 'Just hold your peace . . .'

Just then Meadowsweet and Teasel came marching into the meeting hall, their arms filled with documents and books. They looked annoyed, for historians need complete silence to do their important research.

'Must this meeting be so noisy?' complained

Meadowsweet. 'We can't hear ourselves think in the library.'

'She's ultra-sensitive to sound, you see,' grinned Teasel. 'A bit like a bat. I always tiptoe around the bookshelves in case I disturb her. In fact, she's writing another epic poem. She's been scribbling for days, and muttering about knobbly knees for some reason.'

'Actually, it's not a poem, it's an ode,' said the girl, casting him a chilly glance. 'I have called it "Ode to the Grasshopper".'

'And it's very good,' smiled Teasel. 'Made even more brilliant by the extraordinary length of it. Thirty-five verses and she's still not finished!'

Meadowsweet smiled sweetly at the audience. 'Perhaps while the clan is gathered together they'd like to hear a snatch of it?'

And ignoring the giggles and groans, she mounted the dais, shoving Nettles and Poppy aside as she unrolled a thick parchment. Then, in her high clear voice, she read, 'Ode to the Grasshopper' and launched into it . . .

'Morning long I lay at ease
Gazing at his knobbly knees,
Oh the tension of those hours
Sprawled amongst the scented flowers,
Would I see the main attraction,
Would I view those knees in action?
Zip, he sprang too fast to see,
Mocking poor bedazzled me.'

She bowed, blushing with pleasure as polite applause rippled around the hall. Then she became tearful as she explained, 'The last verse will be very sad. It's about when I finally see the grasshopper's knees in action. But by that time his joints are creaky with age, and he can't zip so fast any more . . . please excuse my distress . . .'

'I never guessed it would end like that,' soothed Teasel, patting her heaving shoulders. 'We could have wept together, had you told me. That's what comes of ignoring my opinions.'

'Another of your cruel taunts, I suppose,' snapped Meadowsweet, shrugging him away.

'No wonder I try to ignore you. And if you ever speak to me again, I'll be even more ignorant.'

'Impossible,' grinned Teasel. 'Your "Ode to the Grasshopper" will go down in our clan history as the ode that plumbed the depths of genius. Ignorance has nothing to do with it.'

'Apology accepted,' said Meadowsweet, primly. Then she turned back to the audience, her quill pen poised to take down notes. 'Now, good people, as your official historian I'm interested to know what this meeting is all about. Please tell me in your own simple words, and I'll jot them down.'

'I'd like to know why Nettles and Poppy are standing on the leader's dais,' said puzzled Teasel. 'They're usually in Granny Willow's kitchen. Are they up here pleading for mercy because they've burnt our lunchtime stew, or something?'

'My days of stirring stews are over,' cried Nettles, elbowing Teasel and Meadowsweet aside. 'For your history books, I've just been proclaimed as the new leader of the Willow Clan. This valley is about to be invaded by ruffian warriors from the north, and I've been chosen to hurl them back, should they storm our valley beach!'

'But then hot news never travels well through quiet libraries,' said Poppy, tartly. 'I suppose bookworms have always been hard of hearing.'

'A kitchen-boy and -girl, strutting before our eyes,' said Meadowsweet, amazed. 'Does it mean we'll have no lunch today?'

'Who cares about lunch,' teased Teasel, 'when one can gaze at pretty Poppy. Perhaps you should try your hand at peeling vegetables, Meadowsweet.'

'I'm not standing here for decoration,' snapped angry Poppy. 'Preparing vegetables was a mere preparation for my standing here at the side of Nettles, his loyal companion for life.'

'Me too,' chirped Jenny. 'For I know when I've backed a winner.'

'So Finn our old leader is no more,' mused Teasel, sadly. 'See how he stands amongst the audience as if he doesn't matter. And weeping

Pansy too. I hope there's nothing fishy going on.'

'I can certainly smell fish,' said Meadowsweet, her delicate nostrils flaring.

'Fish did play a part in Finn's downfall,' said Nettles, defiantly. 'Though admiring him as we do, he had become so addicted to fishing that he failed to learn about the invaders' ship that's rowing towards our valley.'

'Too much casting his net in muddy backwaters,' sighed Poppy, 'egged on by Pansy, who has also lost her sense of duty to the Willow Clan.'

Pansy was just about to leap on to the dais to attack Poppy, when the door at the back of the hall burst open yet again. A fearsome sight stood there. It was Granny Willow brandishing her steaming spoon and looking angrier than ever. She didn't mince her words as she shouted at the cringing crowd.

'Are you coming in to lunch, or what? My stew must be eaten while it's hot. I demand that you stop this meeting and get some nourishment down you. You can prattle about foolish things all you want afterwards. But I'm not sweating in my kitchen just to have my recipes ignored. I'm not cooking for folk who don't appreciate my efforts!'

'And neither are we!' cried Rosie and Thorn, her tired new trainees. They were carrying a huge cauldron of stew between them while trying to balance stacks of bowls on their heads. Despite the slavery their new jobs entailed, they looked happy enough. For hadn't they stepped on to the first rung of the ladder that led to success? Of course, they would flee the steamy kitchen when fame came. But for now they were content to slave under Granny Willow's kind authority.

'You've no right to interrupt this meeting, Granny Willow,' said Nettles, annoyed. 'It is extremely important. It could mean the life or the death of our clan, in fact the fate of our whole valley!'

'Play your silly war-games if you must,' cried the irate lady. 'But play them after meals. In the meantime my stew is getting cold.'

'Granny Willow is not amused,' whispered the audience as the old lady stormed away. 'We're lucky we didn't get rapped on the head by her spoon!'

'Very well,' said Nettles. 'To calm Granny Willow this meeting will take a short lunch break. And there'll be no wasting time clamouring for second helpings. I want you all back here as soon as possible.'

'And while Nettles is eating his lunch he must not be disturbed,' said Poppy, firmly. 'He and I will dine alone to allow his plans to mature inside his head. If anyone approaches, I'll send them away with a flea in their ear. That snub applies to everyone, no matter how brilliant their own ideas might be.'

'Don't you dare snub me,' said Jenny, indignantly. 'Don't forget we're a team of three, close companions for life.'

'The snub will apply to everyone but Jenny,' agreed Poppy. 'Now let's all go into lunch before Granny Willow blows her top.'

'A proper little tyrant young Nettles is becoming,' murmured an elder as the clan filed into the dining room. 'It makes one pine for the calmness of Finn. But leaders must come and go. That is the way of the world.'

'Our Poppy is also becoming overbearing,' frowned another. 'And she was so shy and sweet just yesterday. But she'll sensibly settle down, I'm certain of it.'

'Ambition and power,' said a third, sadly. 'Such desires can so easily turn the heads of the young. Especially the heads of the lowly ones. I suppose that washing dishes and chopping vegetables makes them more determined to make their mark in life.'

Soon the clan was seated around the rough wooden tables wolfing down bowls of delicious stew with hunks of acorn bread. Granny Willow watched contentedly as her recipe was spooned down to sighs of delight. For herself, she wasn't concerned about the valley being invaded by a bristling ship. It was probably someone's imagination anyway. She had plenty of problems of her own to cope with. The main one was making sure that the clan was properly fed. Regular mealtimes were more important to her than figments of wild imaginations. Her ideal was to have mealtimes as exactly on time as the rising and the setting of the sun. She ignored Nettles' order that there should be no time-wasting second helpings. Assisted by Rosie and Thorn she dipped her deep spoon into the cauldron to refill the bowls of the still ravenous souls. Earlier that day the old lady had not been amused, but now she was happy and laughing as she fed her family with every last drop of stew.

And then amidst a clattering of bowls and benches it was back to the meeting hall . . .

Four

TO JOURNEY IN HOPE

'Will you all please stop burping,' shouted Nettles. 'After much thought over lunch I've arrived at a plan. In my opinion, the best form of defence is attack. Therefore, with my warriors around me I intend to charge the invaders the moment they attempt to wade ashore. With that tactic we'll quickly hurl them back into the waves.'

'In short, we'll fight them on the beaches,' cried Poppy. 'Before they have time to find their landlubber legs.'

'While they're still staggering about,' grinned Jenny. 'Because of the huge amounts of ale they all glug down.'

'Which can only result in blood being spilled on both sides,' said a gentle voice. It was Sage. Encouraged by the sudden silence she spoke on. 'It isn't derring-do we need, but wisdom. Wise council is more effective than rash violence if sought and listened to.'

'It's action we need,' argued Nettles. 'We know that you aren't a coward, Sage. We all witnessed your bravery during our quest for the end of the tail. But our valley is in danger of being destroyed. Anyway, whose wisdom can we call upon with time running out so quickly? We can't ask Robin and Fern because they're both rather doddery in their old age, and we certainly can't turn to Finn who's become addicted to lazy fishing these days.'

'Nor Pansy, who's also a slave to Finn's habit,' said Poppy, quickly. 'I say we should put wisdom aside and attack the foreign ship defensively as Nettles outlined in his grand plan.'

'I'd like to hear more about Sage's wisdom idea,' shouted someone from the crowd. 'The plan Nettles suggests sounds dangerous to me. There's no serious thought behind it. He could lead us to certain death amongst the swinging axes of the invaders if we go along with him. Let's hear more from steady-minded Sage. Her opinions are always sensible.'

'I think I can read the mind of our plump, muddy vole,' grinned Jenny. 'She's thinking about a certain someone who lives further upstream in a briar patch beside a pond. Who smarms and smiles, and peddles phoney magic guiles.'

'Who would that certain someone be?' shouted the intrigued audience. Even the elders who had been enjoying their after-lunch naps woke up to listen.

'None other than Berrybottom of The Briars,'

chuckled Jenny. 'A small wizard so wise that his parents dismissed him as a fool the moment he uttered his first words. A third-rate wizard himself, his father tried to drown him in the family pond. But the young Berrybottom was so full of windy words that he kept bobbing to the surface. The old Berrybottom gave up in despair and died, while his mother ran home to her parents, leaving young Berrybottom an orphan. Now, even till this day, he squats in squalor beside his pond, selling wise nonsense and quack magic potions to anyone foolish enough to be taken in by his wily charms. I always avoid him myself.'

'Poor Berrybottom of The Briars,' sighed a soft-hearted lady. 'Living all alone in a briar patch beside a pond. How sad and lonely his life must be.'

'Berrybottom, sad?' scoffed Jenny. 'Cunning is the word. He's spent his life cheating folk out of their valuables and gold. As for being lonely, he's had three wives already. And got rid of them in some mysterious fashion. He's probably marrying another one even as we speak!'

'Why does he marry so many wives?' asked a puzzled lady. 'Does he constantly change the old one for a new one?'

'Because like a fool he always marries wives who nag him day and night,' said Jenny. 'He's too stupid to learn from his mistakes and stay single. So much for the wisdom of that silly wizard.'

'Berrybottom has a devoted following,' protested Sage. 'His magic might go wrong from time to time but his flashes of genius are legendary. An aunt of mine once went to him complaining that her life was totally black. When she left her head was swimming with bright colours and happiness. She still swears by his magic mushroom broth!'

'I also have a tale to tell about friend Berrybottom,' grimaced Jenny. 'A pal of mine sought his help. Her beak was beginning to twist to the left and she wanted it straightened. As she had no gold, Berrybottom demanded some of her tail feathers in payment. He said he needed them for a special spell he was brewing. My pal, desperate for treatment, agreed to his outrageous price. The result was that after lots of mumbo-jumbo she was chased away with her beak twisted to the right and her tail feathers cruelly snatched out! So much for the healing talents of that phoney wizard, eh? So much for the scoundrel who ruined the life of my pal and gave her a nervous breakdown. So I warn you, Nettles, steer clear of Berrybottom of The Briars. His magic and wisdom will always be the ramblings of a fool, in love with gold and his own selfish self.'

'Yet Berrybottom's flashes of genius can't be denied, Nettles,' urged Sage. 'It surely won't hurt to visit him, to hear what he makes of our problem. Who knows, he might come up with the wise advice we need to settle the invader crisis in a peaceful way. We at least owe it to our innocent families to try. I still believe that Berrybottom is a gifted genius, even if a flawed one.'

'I think you're right, Sage,' mused Nettles. 'We'll take a trip upstream and visit this

Berrybottom of yours. I've never talked with a fellow genius before.'

'He'll never be a genius of your equal, Nettles,' murmured Poppy, adoringly.

'Come on, let's go and swap stupidities then,' said disgusted Jenny, 'leading to blunders which will end up who knows where. I'll only say that I'm still yours to command, my leader. Though forgive me if my patience wears thin from time to time.'

'Sage,' ordered Nettles. 'Prepare for a trip upstream. How many can you ferry?'

'Perhaps a party of four at a squeeze,' said the eager vole. 'Allowing for currents and undertows.'

'Then there's no time to lose,' shouted Nettles, leaping from the dais and striding from the hall. He was hurriedly followed by Poppy and Jenny as well as Meadowsweet and Teasel, who insisted that as librarians they were needed to record history in the making. As they strode past Granny Willow's kitchen the old lady poked her head through the clouds of steam.

'Just remember to be back in time for supper,' she shrilled. 'Tonight it's shrimp stew courtesy of Finn, garnished with my secret herbs.'

'If we're late just keep it warm, Granny Willow,' said Nettles, sternly. 'At the moment we've more important things to think about than stew.'

'Never forget you started out as a humble washer-upper,' cried the lady, tears streaming down her lined cheeks as the boy swaggered away. 'And if you fail to measure up as a hero, don't expect to get your old job back. So walk away, just break my heart with not a goodbye, if you must!'

Nettles stopped and turned. Fondly he said, 'You'll always be in my heart, Granny Willow. Come fame or failure, I'll always come hurrying home for a bowl of your warming stew . . .' then he and his party quickly departed to swarm down the oak to the bank of the stream below.

'How grand it must be to strut in the limelight,' sighed envious Rosie and Thorn, her new helpers.

'When fame comes to us we'll also call home for a bowl of your famous stew, Granny Willow!'

'Never mind about your foolish dreams,' scolded the lady. 'We've tonight's supper to worry about. The shrimps are simmering nicely in my cauldron. In the meantime have you popped in the vegetables, and are the stew bowls thoroughly rinsed?'

'We'll go and check, Granny Willow,' said the pair, scurrying back into the stifling and steamy kitchen.

The spring evening air was cool but still bright as Sage coasted away from the bank of the stream, her passengers secure on her broad back. Soon she was paddling with powerful paws, fighting the swift waters that sought to sweep her down to the sea. Above the sailing party flitted Jenny, sometimes darting ahead from twig to twig, her eyes alert for danger. Then suddenly she was zipping back to Sage and her spray-soaked passengers. Gasping for breath she announced that their destination was just around the next bend. She also had some tittle-tattle to tell – it seemed that since her last spying mission on Berrybottom he had taken a new wife, his fourth. Her name, said the grinning bird, was Crabapple.

'Berrybottom should be in a good mood then,' said Nettles, relieved. 'A genius is much more stable with someone to fetch and carry for him.'

'I wouldn't count on it,' warned Jenny, as Sage glided into shore. 'I listened by the pond for a while and all I could hear was Crabapple nagging and complaining and Berrybottom meekly saying "Yes, dear" in total obedience.'

'So Berrybottom has made another wedding mistake,' said Poppy, shaking her head. 'A nagging wife called Crabapple doesn't sound very promising for his future happiness, nor for our mission.'

'No promise at all,' agreed Jenny. 'The blushing bride sounds as bitter as her name. I warned you not to come. But you all preferred to listen to Sage instead.'

'We must not judge too soon,' said Meadowsweet, clambering ashore and following the party along the slippery path through the trees. 'Even crabapples sweeten with age. Is Berrybottom's new wife very old, Jenny wren?'

'Very much so,' shuddered the bird. 'And wrinkly with it.'

'Then her sweetness must lie within,' said confident Meadowsweet. 'One should never judge a book by its cover, as Teasel does. In fact I've a mind to write a poem about the bitter-sweetness of life.'

'But not now, eh?' urged Teasel, grabbing the sleeve of her tunic as she slipped in the mud. 'For the moment just watch where you're putting your dainty feet.'

And so with Sage in the lead the party slithered along the track that snaked through the trees. Finally in a clearing they caught their first glimpse of the home of the fabled wizard, Berrybottom of

The Briars. Before they had time to look properly their ears were assaulted by the most raucous singing they had ever heard. It was blasting out from a briar patch beside a small, calm pond which glowed strangely golden as waters never did. As if its depths concealed some secret from the curious world . . .

> 'Berrybottom is my name,
> Spells and wisdom are my game,
> I'm the idol of the ladies,
> Berrybottom is my name . . .'

'Shut that racket!' screamed a voice from a flickering fire beside the pond. 'Your days of chasing ladies are over, Berrybottom. Stirring spells and thinking up wise advice, that's your job. I married you to get rich, not poor. Just concentrate on thinking up some gold-spinning projects. You promised I'd drip with gold on my wedding day. Well, I'm still waiting!'

'Sorry, Crabapple,' replied the singer, meekly.

'The song just burst out of me. I'll never sing again if it makes you unhappy. You know you're very precious to me . . .'

At those words the sound of weird cackling laughter came from the thick undergrowth. Through the greenery three indistinct and ghostly shapes could be seen. They appeared to be performing some ritual, circular dance. Then the three pale figures began to chant. The chant was low and muffled and filled with sinister chuckles. It was not a song of love, but rather a hymn of hate. And judging by the name the pale singers spat out, it was aimed at the wizard of The Briars himself . . . namely Berrybottom.

At that moment Nettles and his nervous party stepped from the trees and advanced towards the pond . . .

Five

BERRYBOTTOMS DOWN THE AGES

There had always been Berrybottoms in the Valley of the People. Legend told that the first Berrybottom wandered into the valley quite by chance. His only possessions were a pot, a flint for making fire and a large pouch slung over his shoulder stuffed with various bits and bobs that had caught his eye along the way. These became the ingredients for future spells when he set up in business as a wizard. After his long walk he took a fancy to a sprawl of briar bushes that grew beside a small pond deep in a wood. From this base he began to brew healing potions to peddle to the clans of People already beginning to drift into the valley to build their homes and lives. He also sold wise advice as a sideline, for wizards were expected to be wise.

The snag was that Berrybottom's spells and advice rarely worked. His customers often found themselves with more problems than they had started with, so his reputation as a clever wizard began to plunge. His trade dwindled away to almost nothing. But one magic power never failed him.

In spite of being ugly and scruffy, he could charm the ladies. He could always cast a spell over them. So he quickly married, but alas, it didn't work out. Snapdragon, his wife, quickly began to nag him about never earning enough gold to make them rich. Soon she was nagging about every little thing.

'Why don't you take a regular plunge in the pond to get rid of your fleas?' she complained.

'Because bathing destroys the natural oils in the body,' replied Berrybottom the Elder. 'Every good wizard knows that.'

'Then at least smarten yourself up,' she nagged, 'instead of being constantly scruffy. No wonder we're losing customers!'

'Clothes do not maketh the wizard,' replied stubborn Berrybottom.

'And why do you always scratch yourself raw when I try to reason with you?' snapped Snapdragon. 'And grimace with a long face when I try to improve your image?'

'I don't know the reason for that,' said Berrybottom, darkly. 'But I'm on my way to working it out. Perhaps it's because you're beginning to nag too much.'

Then came the time when Berrybottom could bear no more of Snapdragon's griping. He was now anxious to be rid of her, for he had already cast a charming spell over another maiden whom he intended to make wife number two. But how to get rid of Snapdragon? This was the thorny problem he faced as he crouched all alone in his briar patch. Peering out he could see her huddled over the fire by the pond, muttering about his failures as usual. The sight hardened Berrybottom's heart. For a long time he brooded and thought. Then came the idea that would turn his life of misery into one of perfect happiness, if it worked. He would invent a spell that would make Snapdragon vanish from the face of the earth for ever! But what ingredients would he need to do the dastardly deed? He decided to experiment. He would rely on the trusted method of trial and error.

So at the wizardly hour of midnight, Berrybottom the Elder crept from the briars and began to roam far and wide. Many hours he spent gathering bits of this and snippets of that which he stuffed inside his pouch. Snail slime was silver-bright and easy to spot by moonlight. So were the jellied strings of toadspawn in the mirror-black pools that he passed. And there were lots of glowing mushrooms in the wood that made the head spin if sniffed too deeply. After a search lasting many nights, Berrybottom was sure that he had all the magic ingredients that would make nagging Snapdragon vanish for ever. And then came the time for testing.

One evening Berrybottom mixed some ingredients in his pot with a drop of water, adding a dollop of cuckoo-spit to blend it. Then he crawled from his briar hide, put the pot on the fire and began to stir. As it started to bubble he waved his gnarled hands over the brew and began to chant strange words. Snapdragon, who was sitting on the other side of the fire, became suspicious. She was always wary of Berrybottom experimenting with new spells that she knew nothing about.

'What's that you're cooking up?' she snapped. 'Another of your useless potions, I suppose. And what is that chant you're muttering? I haven't heard that one before.'

She soon found out. All at once she began to feel dizzy, as if she was drifting away from the world, or the world was drifting away from her. Berrybottom watched with great interest as her temper-flushed face began to fade to a whiter shade of pale. Slowly she began to take on a ghostly appearance, as if she was neither here nor anywhere else. She was fading away, there was no doubt about it!

'Before you vanish completely,' said delighted Berrybottom, 'I'd like to say goodbye, dear.'

But as usual Berrybottom's spell turned out flawed. For Snapdragon remained only half-vanished. White as snow and like a wraith she rose and railed at her wicked husband. Then, as if in a dream, she drifted off into the woods, into the limbo-world where his spell had cast her. For a long time she would wander alone cursing Berrybottom with all her heart.

As for her heartless husband, he quickly married the maiden he had been eyeing for some time. Her name was Sourplum. But when she too began to nag him he swiftly spelled her, to share the fate of Snapdragon. His third wife Bitterroot also went into the wilderness, after she had dared to push Berrybottom into the pond to wash him clean of grime and fleas. But she left something behind that Berrybottom would treasure till his dying day – a son, Berrybottom the second. A boy he would raise in his own image. A lad who would one day take over The Briars and the pond. Who would become a wizard of spells and potions and wise advice. And also an expert ridder of nagging wives.

And so the Berrybottoms lived and died. They took little notice of their cast-off wives shouting curses from the woods as they flitted through the trees like ghosts. But the Berrybottoms did begin to pay nervous notice when the spurned wives began to taunt that they were working on a vanishing spell of their own. A spell that would vanish and end the line of Berrybottom for ever. Fearfully they stepped up their search to discover the perfect vanishing spell before the ghostly wives did it first. But through the generations it had proved impossible, for it seemed there was always one vital ingredient that eluded them. And so it became a race against time. Who would find that vital ingredient first? A Berrybottom, or a bitter ex-wife?

And so the warring situation remained until the present day . . .

Six

THE OUTRAGEOUS PRICE OF ADVICE

As the party advanced across the clearing, the scene that met their eyes was both beautiful and squalid. The waters of the pond glowed strangely golden, perhaps an effect of the sun, while the encircling birch trees gleamed silver-bright as the spring day began to die. But the unsightly piles of refuse spoiled what could have been an ideal beauty spot. An air of decay and a buzzing swarm of bluebottles hung over the home of Berrybottom of The Briars. There was certainly no silver in the tone of the voice that harshly greeted their arrival.

'Who goes there?' it bawled, causing the travellers to jump.

Was it the voice of the fabled Berrybottom himself? If not, it could only be that of Crabapple, his latest wife. It seemed to sound from the direction of the dismally flickering fire beside the pond. Then the voice snapped out again, making the visitors jump a second time.

'What do you want, and what will you pay for it?' the voice demanded. 'If you need a spell or a potion it will cost you twice as much gold on account of the lateness of the day. Berrybottom always demands a double bonus at sunset. On the other hand, if you've come begging for wise advice it'll cost you even more. In fact, triple the daytime price because Berrybottom's brain becomes strained when the sun goes down. He finds it hard to be brilliant when his mind begins to cool. And remember, he only accepts gold as payment for his services these days. A rule that started from the day when he fell in love and married me. So payment in nail-clippings and tail feathers is no longer acceptable, if that's what you've come to offer. The sport of cheating Berrybottom is over. But here comes my husband now. And remember, I'll be listening closely. So don't even dream of trying to cheat him!'

The nervous and silent party watched as a figure came crawling from the depths of a tangled mass of briar bushes. He then loped towards the visitors and slumped down on his haunches in a slick of mud. He looked a picture of misery as he stared at them through dull eyes that constantly darted towards the hunched shape crouched by the fire. If this was the wizard Berrybottom, mixer of potions and giver of wise advice, he hardly looked the part. And for a newly-wed he seemed very downcast. He wore a ragged grey tunic and hose, clumsily fashioned from the leaves of an especially itchy plant that must have been agony to wear. And all the while he winced and scratched himself as if plagued by small creatures he knew, or by some demon he didn't. Only once did his brown eyes light up, when he noticed Poppy and Meadowsweet.

'What lovely ladies,' he smiled, showing a row of craggy teeth. 'And wearing such pretty hats.'

Poppy and Meadowsweet were appalled to be addressed in such a familiar manner by this smelly and scruffy person. Then Berrybottom's face fell grim again as his grimy fingers found some new, itchy spot to scratch. The opinion of the party was that Berrybottom the wizard was not a happily married person, which, from their point of view, was unusual. Noticing his snub, upturned nose it was plain that he was of the People. And the People were known to marry happily and for life . . .

'Berrybottom of The Briars, I presume?' said Nettles, stepping forward warily. 'I believe your good lady wife has already introduced herself.'

'Then you know that my skills don't come

cheap any more,' said Berrybottom. 'My new wife is now in charge of everything, including me and my prices. So what can I do for you, welcome customers?'

'We'd like to buy some advice, please,' answered Nettles, politely. 'We belong to the Willow Clan and we live in a great oak tree a little way downstream. At this moment we're worrying about a certain ship that's sailing towards this valley. The Jenny wren perched on that twig by your ear has warned us that the ship is crammed with fierce warriors from a faraway land, all waving sharp axes and threatening to do terrible things. We intend to resist them, but we're not sure what to do. So we'd be grateful for your wise advice on the matter. By the way, I'm Nettles, the new leader of the Willow Clan.'

'Which means you'll be in charge of your clan's gold,' grinned Berrybottom, eagerly rubbing his grubby hands. 'And lots of it, I hope. Because I must warn you that one piece of advice will do you no good. In your desperate state you'll need three pieces of advice which will be very expensive. Have you enough gold on you to pay my triple prices? As Crabapple says, I don't come cheap any more.'

'We haven't much gold on us,' admitted Nettles. 'Just a few personal trinkets. But I'm sure we can meet your price with the help of our worried family and friends.'

'Berrybottom demands the full amount, and no less,' yelled Crabapple from her fireside. 'We won't accept your trinkets with the rest spread out till the end of the world! Watch them, Berrybottom, they look a cunning bunch to me. Stick up for your rights unless you wish to start looking for a new wife!'

'Yes dear, I mean, no dear,' replied Berrybottom, clawing at an itchy ear.

'As Nettles said, we'll raise the gold,' said Poppy, desperately. 'Our clan will donate all they have to save the lives of the valley folk.'

'And Umber and Amber and their Guardian Clan will surely chip in,' said confident

Meadowsweet. 'I'm certain they'll donate all the riches they have for the sake of the valley and their Great Golden Snake who is sleeping at the moment.'

'And you could throw in a few of your golden verses,' grinned Teasel. 'They must be worth more than their weight in gold.'

'As a last resort, perhaps,' sniffed Meadowsweet.

'What shall I do, Crabapple dear?' called Berrybottom over his shoulder. 'It seems they can't pay immediately.'

'Then double-triple the price of each piece of advice, you fool,' yelled the hag from her fire. 'You're supposed to be a wizard, so alarm them. Threaten to turn them all into toads if they can't pay the full amount by tomorrow. Which, according to my sums, is three sackfuls of high quality gold.'

'That's the deal,' sighed Berrybottom, scratching his armpit vigorously. 'Crabapple has spoken, so take it or leave it. The whole amount of gold to be paid in full by tomorrow.'

'I promise we'll meet your price,' said anxious Nettles. 'Now will you please give us the three pieces of advice we desperately need, for time is running out for our valley while we argue.'

'Oh, for pity's sake, Berrybottom,' snapped Jenny. 'Stop scratching for a moment and give us your advice, for what it's worth.'

Berrybottom lowered his shaggy head into his hands and began to ponder. He seemed to be waiting for the wisdom to come surging into his brain. Now and then his body gave a jerky tremor. But that was probably the fleas taking up new positions on his ravaged skin.

'Please put us out of our misery, Berrybottom,' pleaded Meadowsweet. Meanwhile Teasel just looked on, his grin ever widening. As for Sage, the champion of the wizard of The Briars, she grew more anxious as time passed. Then suddenly . . .

'The wisdom is coming through!' cried Berrybottom, rousing from his ponderings. 'My first piece of advice is that you should flee for your lives when the invaders arrive.'

Nettles was horrified and angry. Never would he commit such a cowardly act! He said so in no uncertain terms. Berrybottom was unmoved by his outburst.

'My second piece of advice is that you should stand and fight,' he said. 'In fact sacrifice your lives for your valiant cause.'

Nettles brightened. That was more like it! It was exactly his own plan. It was what true warriors were trained to do. He and his party waited with bated breath for the last piece of advice.

'Finally,' said Berrybottom, scraping back his fringe of matted hair, 'my third piece of advice is that you should stand on the shore and shift from foot to foot as the invaders come sailing in. This will throw them into confusion. They won't know whether you intend to stand and fight, or run away. Your undecided actions will convince the invaders that they've gone completely mad. Then all you'll need to do is to round up the whole bewildered bunch and ship 'em back where they belong. And that's the end of your problem.'

'But it doesn't make sense,' protested Nettles.

'Wise advice rarely does,' shrugged Berrybottom. 'But it'll still cost you three full sacks of gold.'

'We're not paying good gold for bad advice,' cried angry Poppy.

'Be turned into toads then,' yelled Crabapple from her fire. 'The great wizard Berrybottom can do things you'd never dream of.'

'I don't want to be a toad,' wept Meadowsweet. 'I couldn't bear to look like Teasel.'

'Give me a kiss and I'll be your prince,' grinned Teasel.

'Oh, the horror of it,' shuddered Meadowsweet.

'You did promise to pay,' said Berrybottom, worried. 'If Crabapple says you must, then you must. She's my new wife you see, and she likes her own way.'

'Very well, we'll pay your price somehow,' said

Nettles, reluctantly. 'Even though your advice is quite useless.'

It was obvious that the journey upstream had been a waste of precious time. As the new leader of the clan, Nettles accepted that the blame was his. But for a while he seemed uncertain what to do, probably because of his extreme youth and inexperience. In the meantime Jenny hopped impatiently on her twig, while Sage sighed regretfully. It was Poppy who pointed out that the night was drawing on, and they should be setting off for home. Nettles grasped that sensible advice and agreed.

'We're urgently needed back home, Berrybottom,' he explained. 'But before we go could we strike some bargain? You can have all our trinkets of gold right now. On top of that you'll have my honourable promise that we'll pay you the rest of the huge amount as soon as we can raise it.'

'No, we won't strike such a bargain,' shrilled Crabapple. 'We demand the full price of three sackfuls of gold all at once. And to make sure we get it I'm ordering Berrybottom to go with you, to haunt your shadows even to the ends of the earth. We'll have our three sackfuls of gold even if Berrybottom dies in the attempt to get what's ours. Do you hear me, Berrybottom? I want you to stick like a leech to those slippery customers and bring back the riches you promised me. And don't be fobbed off with the glitter of false fools' gold!'

'I hear you, dear,' said Berrybottom, meekly.

'And if you don't come back with the gold, then don't come back at all,' she yelled. 'I can always find a new husband to worship me. I certainly don't intend to end up like your other wives who cackle and chant and flit through the trees around our home as if a spell has been cast upon them. If you're that magnetic and charming I've yet to see it.'

'So, if I'm not back tomorrow with three sacks of gold then you'll divorce me?' asked Berrybottom, his grubby fingers crossed. 'You'll run away and find a better husband?'

'That is my intention,' snapped Crabapple. 'So now you know what you need to do to keep me as your loving wife.'

'Yes, Crabapple dear,' said Berrybottom, his dull eyes beginning to sparkle. 'I'll be back tomorrow with the gold. Though it might be the day after, or even next week. Will you wait for me if I'm a bit late coming home to The Briars?'

'Tomorrow is your deadline,' cried Crabapple. 'One moment later and I'm gone!'

No longer was Berrybottom the dejected wizard of earlier. He fairly bounced on his grimy bare toes to his briar-bush lair to gather together a few personal items. Then he nervously approached the fire where his glowering wife was sitting. Snatching up his spell-pot he came scampering back to the party, ready and eager to travel.

He was not the only one wishing to get away from that dismal place. But there was one small girl who was in no hurry at all. Ignoring the urging of everyone to leave well alone, she marched forward into the light from the flickering fire. Bravely she returned the harsh stare of Crabapple with a smile. The small poetess was determined to see goodness in the cold heart of Berrybottom's wife.

'I don't believe you're as nasty as you sound,' she said. 'I'm certain that deep down you're really quite nice. And I've composed a small poem to prove it.' Then in her piping voice she began to quote . . .

'So grimly did the crabapple
Cling to her frosty bough,
Till bitterly she fell to earth . . .
Behold her sweetness now.'

'Sweet, am I?' screamed Crabapple. 'Who can be sweet in this bitter world? My parents were bitter, their parents were bitter, and I'm the most bitter of all! Once I was a sweet young thing dreaming of marrying a rich and loving husband. And I ended up with that Berrybottom, for ever scratching himself and as poor as a pauper can be. I thought I'd married an ambitious charmer, not a failure. I'll show you how sweet I am, foolish girl. Be gone before I roast you on my fire with chestnuts for my supper . . .' and she leapt from her fireside and dashed at the girl, her bony fingers poised to throttle. The fury on her face told all. Shocked and sobbing, Meadowsweet raced back to the safety of her friends as Crabapple's threats rang around the clearing.

'Quick!' shouted Nettles. 'Everyone back down to the stream. Crabapple has lost control and could injure someone!'

The party needed no urging. They were already fleeing helter-skelter back along the muddy path that led down to the water. Winging behind came Jenny, her eyes sparkling with mirth. She had noticed that Berrybottom had been the first one to bolt when his wife gave vent to her rage. Theirs was a perfect example of hasty love turned sour.

Soon Sage was slipping back into the stream to ferry the party home. The journey back to the oak proved tiring, burdened as she was with the overload of Berrybottom. But there was no shortage of helpers. Nettles was becoming a natural leader, as he shouted out sensible orders. While he and Poppy paddled with their hands, Meadowsweet and Teasel dived overboard to grasp Sage's fur, helping her to negotiate the treacherous rocks and rapids. Berrybottom refused to help. He crouched on Sage's back, trembling and glancing over his shoulder, fearful that Crabapple had changed her mind and was in hot pursuit to order him back home. Above them in the now moonlit sky flitted Jenny. She was pleased with herself. Hadn't she warned that the trip upstream would be a waste of time? Now everyone knew she was right, though none said it as the party neared the home oak.

The only person who was enjoying the trip was Berrybottom. Clutching his spell-pot and three empty gold sacks, with his ingredients pouch slung over his shoulder, he was looking happier and happier as the distance between him and

Crabapple increased. But he wasn't yet out of his woods of worry. For suddenly from the trees along the bank of the stream echoed a cackling chant . . .

> 'We the wives of Berrybottom
> Cast off by his marrying whim,
> Pray this spell will do its duty,
> Let our stirrings do for him.'

From their limbo-world of neither here nor there, his ex-wives were determined upon the downfall of Berrybottom. Having learned much about his secret ingredients they were busily working on their own spell to make him vanish – completely. They too were urgently seeking the missing ingredient that would make the spell work perfectly. Slipping from tree to tree, they followed the progress of the party.

'Prepare to meet your doom, false Berrybottom,' cried the ghostly figure of Nightshade from the shore.

'From Hell you came, and to Hell you'll return,' shrieked Leafmould, his second discarded wife.

'With not a grave to mark your disappearance,' yelled Sourseed, his third. 'A single puff of smoke will end the wickedness of the Berrybottoms.'

'Leave me alone, you old hags,' shouted fearful Berrybottom. 'I'm off in search of true happiness with my new friends. I intend to start a new life. Why would you deny me a fresh start, an old leaf turned over?'

'Because your old leaf ruined our lives,' chorused the three wives from their whiter shade of pale world. 'Turn over your new leaf if you will, but we'll always turn it back to the wicked chapters you'd like to forget. For your days are numbered, Berrybottom of The Briars. We three wives are now very close to discovering the secret recipe of your vanishing spell which only half-worked. The time is nearing when we'll brew and stir and curse over the correct mixture. Then it's goodbye, Berrybottom. For you'll be vanished without trace for ever and ever.'

'Not if I discover the secret ingredient first,' cried the frightened wizard of The Briars. 'Then I'll show you nagging lot how I'll vanish *you* without a trace!'

Soon the cackling voices and the fleeting ghost figures faded as Sage and her toiling friends coasted around the final bend in the stream. Berrybottom's shouting and bobbing up and down on Sage's back had annoyed everyone, especially as he had not attempted to help during the journey.

'Now you've finished talking to the trees,' said angry Nettles, 'you might be interested to know that we've arrived back at our home oak with not a finger of help from you.'

'Is this where you store all your gold?' asked Berrybottom, clutching his three empty gold sacks to his chest. His eyes were glistening with greed as he gazed up at the towering oak tree, while Sage glided in to shore.

'How can you lust after gold at such a time,' said contemptuous Poppy, 'when our valley is in danger of being destroyed! And it's your valley too, you unfeeling Berrybottom of The Briars.'

But the happy wizard seemed not to hear. His grimy face was alight with joy as he threw back his unkempt head and thanked the stars.

'No more nagging, no more of Crabapple's face every morning, noon and night,' he bellowed. 'For Berrybottom has found peace at last, with a promise of lots more gold, and, if my luck holds, a pretty new wife to complete my life. Free at last, free at last, thanks lucky stars, I'm free at last!'

His behaviour thoroughly disgusted Nettles and his weary party as they climbed the rope-ladder into the oak to face the music, to admit the failure of their mission to the waiting Willow Clan . . .

Seven

THE CHARMING BERRYBOTTOM

'A fools' errand, I just knew it,' gloated Pansy. 'Finn would never have made such a pointless journey.'

'Come now, Pansy,' murmured Finn. 'Nettles made an unwise decision. All new leaders make mistakes at first. Success rarely comes immediately.'

'For some leaders it never comes at all,' snapped Poppy. 'For some leaders the only triumphs are fishing trips to catch poor minnows and shrimps.'

The party, soaked and shame-faced, had arrived back at the meeting hall. Nettles was subdued and had nothing to say. While Poppy and Pansy bickered, the bewildered Willow Clan sat waiting for their new leader to act. While they were waiting they had time to stare curiously at the scruffy stranger on the dais, who was busily scratching himself. Being clean people, the clan could only hope that he wasn't crawling with nasty bugs that might hop amongst them. Yet, though he clawed at his red-raw skin, the stranger seemed to be very content and happy. He sat amongst his few possessions – a battered pot, a pouch containing who knew what grisly things and three empty sacks that he clutched to his chest. He was glancing around the crowded hall, smiling a craggy but surprisingly charming smile. The hall was soon buzzing, everyone wondering who he could be.

'This is the self-styled wizard, Berrybottom of The Briars,' said Poppy, sniffily. 'And because of his lust for gold he refuses to go away until we give him three sacks full of it. He insists that it's payment for three bad pieces of advice that he gave us. But in my opinion, he's just a smelly gold-digger who should be ignored.'

'But why does he look so happy?' challenged someone. 'With his dreadful itches and his three empty sacks, what's he got to be happy about?'

Grinning Jenny answered that one. 'He's happy because he's free of his nagging wife. Berrybottom's no longer under Crabapple's thumb, and he likes it very much.'

'Then why does he lust after gold when he's so happy?' asked a puzzled voice. 'We of the Willow Clan have no riches to speak of.'

'I'm afraid our leader Nettles is to blame for that,' sighed Jenny. 'He vowed to pay Berrybottom three sacks of gold for three bad pieces of advice. And if this clan can't pay, then he has the power to vanish you all. Isn't that right, Berrybottom?'

'I'm working on it,' grinned Berrybottom, patting his ingredients. 'It's my anti-wife spell, and I'm close to cracking it.'

This prompted questions from the audience, especially from the ladies. They were intrigued by this rough-and-ready character with the rakish smile.

'If you have such wizardly powers, then turn me into a ravishing beauty,' giggled one lady from the front row. 'Work your powerful magic on me, if you can.'

'What, turn you into a beauty when you are one already?' smiled Berrybottom. 'I couldn't make you prettier for ten sacks of gold!'

The lady blushed to hear such a charming remark. Her friends in the front row agreed that Berrybottom certainly had a way with him. Though it was a pity about his constant scratching, which was a bit off-putting.

'Will you use your powers for a good cause?'

asked someone. 'For instance, will you turn the invaders into toads when their bristling ship comes sailing in?'

'Not without payment,' said Berrybottom, stubbornly. 'I still haven't been paid for the three pieces of advice I sold to Nettles.'

'Apart from lusting for gold, what else do you want from life?' asked another lady, patting her hair and making eyes at him.

'Perhaps a new wife, for a start,' winked Berrybottom. Then for the benefit of all the ladies in the hall he launched into a flirtatious song . . .

> 'Who will keep romance alive,
> Who will be my number five?
> Number four was not my taste,
> Who will take her nagging place?'

Then he spoiled the effect of his flirty song by scratching his itching ears with such fury that they soon glowed a fiery red.

About that time Nettles was rousing from his

thoughtful silence. He rose to his feet and marched to the edge of the dais, holding up his hand for silence.

'I've finally thought everything through,' he announced to relieved cheers. 'I now have all the answers to our problems concerning the approaching ship.'

'How does Nettles do it?' gasped Poppy. 'With all the cares of our valley on his slim shoulders, yet still he looks fresh and noble! How lucky I am to be his sole companion for life.'

'Correction,' snapped Jenny. 'There are three of us in that relationship. Anyway, having answers doesn't mean that they'll work. I hope Nettles has thought of that.'

'Nettles thinks of everything,' said confident Poppy. 'Even his mistakes are carefully thought out. But shush, doubting bird . . .'

'This is the situation, then,' Nettles was saying to the audience. 'As the advice of Berrybottom was useless, I'm falling back on the plan I first suggested – to attack and defeat the enemy on the beaches. But before they arrive we still have time to gather more forces. After this meeting my warriors and I are going to climb Buttercup Hill and share our problems with Umber and Amber of the Guardian Clan. After all, their stake in the peace of this valley is as great as ours. I will ask them to join forces with us to fight off the invaders when they attempt to land upon the beaches of our stream. Now, any questions, and quickly. For time is slipping away and I'm anxious to climb Buttercup Hill where the Great Golden Snake sleeps, to discuss things with Umber and Amber.'

At the word 'golden' Berrybottom's eyes lit up. Scrambling to his feet he snatched for his pot and his pouch of smelly objects. Then, tucking his three sacks under one arm, he announced himself ready to travel to the source of whatever gold was going. But his smile quickly faded as Nettles spoke.

'But the trip up the hill will *not* include Berrybottom,' he said, firmly. 'I'm taking only useful folk on this emergency trip.'

'Berrybottom would only be a pest,' agreed Poppy. 'All he cares about is flirting with the ladies and stuffing his sacks with gold. He doesn't care a jot about saving our valley.'

'At least he has charm,' shouted an angry lady. 'Which is more than Nettles has. And charm might be desperately needed in the desperate days ahead. I believe that the wizard Berrybottom could charm the birds off the trees!'

'Not this bird,' shouted Jenny. But her protest was in vain. Most of the audience were demanding that Berrybottom should be included in the trip.

'Very well,' snapped Nettles. 'He can come with us. So long as he doesn't clamour for gold while we're talking serious business with the Guardians. Now, are there any final questions?'

'Yes,' shouted the ladies at the front. 'Will you swear that Berrybottom will be paid every last scrap of gold that he's owed?'

'I promise,' sighed Nettles. 'Somehow I'll honour his unfair bargain, that's if our valley still exists as we know it.'

His words satisfied Berrybottom's fans. And so the meeting broke up, not least because of the delicious smells wafting from Granny Willow's kitchen. For with the sun long gone and the moon riding high, it was suppertime. And a special suppertime at that. A clan favourite – shrimp stew with secret herbs. What began as an orderly filing from the hall became an eager stampede for the dining hall.

Nettles shook his head in bewilderment. Supper was the last thing on his mind at this terrible time. Stepping from the dais he marched from the hall surrounded by his warriors. They were followed by Meadowsweet and Teasel, the clan historians. Scrambling behind came Berrybottom clutching his possessions. As they passed the kitchen they were waylaid by Granny Willow. She was very sad and angry.

'Why a second mission so hard on the heels of the first?' she cried. 'Haven't you the good manners to stay for supper after all my slaving over it? And you, Nettles, why have you changed so quickly? Why do you choose to ignore me, as if I were a stranger? Am I fading so fast from your heart, you ungrateful boy?'

'I'll never forget you, and my lowly beginnings, Granny Willow,' said Nettles, his words sincere. 'But my life is now full of vital things that need to be done for the sake of our clan. If I succeed in my mission to save our valley, I promise to come back to see you, and to wander through your kitchen for old times' sake. Hopefully my mission in life will not take too long.'

'You'll be home for breakfast then?' said the old lady, delighted. 'I'll prepare your favourite snacks, all piping hot.'

'No, I won't be home for breakfast, Granny Willow,' said the boy, gently. 'For tomorrow is another day. I have so much to do, and so little time to do it in, you see.' Then, squeezing her wrinkled hands, he marched purposefully away.

And in that brief meeting, a grieving Granny Willow realized that she had lost her beloved kitchen-boy for ever. A parting of the ways is often sad, and happens often in life. But sometimes, hopefully, good can come from it. And so it might prove in the lateness of that night . . .

Eight

A Secret Voyage Downstream

As Nettles and his party climbed hurriedly down
the oak and set off for Buttercup Hill, Sage, their
gentle friend, had chosen to stay behind. For she
had whispering words to say to Finn and Pansy,
words that coaxed smiles from their glum faces.
For some time the pair had been feeling quite
useless. Having been branded idle fisherfolk had

distressed them very much, but now the words of Sage had filled them with a sense of worth again.

Soon the trio were also clambering down through the branches of the oak. But their business was different. Their destination was the bank of the stream.

Once there Finn and Pansy boarded Sage's broad back. Then with a flick of her powerful tail she set off on their secret voyage downstream, her whiskered nose cresting the waves, the light from the moon guiding her through the snags and currents. After a long and weaving swim she and her passengers spied what they sought. Sage cruised as near as she dared while they decided on a plan.

It seemed the crew of the northland ship had drawn in their oars, deciding to lie up in this calm cove for the night. The deck of the vessel was ablaze with lantern light and figures could be seen flitting to and fro. On the night air was the sound of raucous laughter and drunken song. The snooping trio were shocked to hear a terrified yell then a splash, as an unfortunate victim was thrown overboard for some crime or other. Then the invaders joined together in song. It was a bloodthirsty chant that made no bones about the fate of those who dared to oppose their power . . .

'Oh, we . . .
Chop them up in a nice rich stew
And we never do feel queasy,
We pop their babies in our pans
And fry them crisp and easy . . .'

Rolling in the gentle swell below, the friends were thinking the awful worst. That evil song could only be a portent of what faced the folk of the valley when the invaders arrived in all their savagery. Something had to be done, and quickly. But what? It was Finn who suggested that they should sneak aboard the ship to hide and watch and listen.

'We need more information,' he whispered. 'We need to see our enemies in the flesh. We need to know about the captain who leads them. Only then will we learn whether they have a chink in their armour that we can exploit.'

'I agree,' hissed Pansy. 'All bullies are cowards at heart. Their brutality is always a mask they use to hide from the things they fear.'

'That will be Finn's chink in their armour,' murmured Sage. 'Hold tight while I glide to the side of the ship to find a good boarding spot.'

Moments later the trio were stealthily climbing the rough-planked side of the ship. Slipping aboard, they concealed themselves inside a large coil of rope. With cautious peeping they were able to see and hear what was going on. And what they saw and heard made them shudder and crouch lower in their hideaway.

The invaders were playing a cruel game of axe-throwing. In the light from the lanterns the watchers could see a small boy lashed to a plank of wood. There was the sound of thudding from sharp axes biting into pine, as the drunken sailors took turns to see how close they could aim their weapons without splitting the quaking boy in two. Then a huge red-haired warrior stepped forward. The others moved aside respectfully. The warrior hefted his axe and swung it in a practice swing.

'What's my name?' he roared at the boy.

'Captain Olaf Ruff,' quavered the small target. 'And please remember that I'm Oswald, your faithful cabin-boy and ship's apprentice.'

'And what am I?' the leader's eyes were icy-blue and coldly unfeeling.

'Ruff by name and rough by nature,' came the faint response. Then hopefully, 'Though as ship's cabin-boy I'm allowed to call you Ollie. And you always call me Ossie when you're in a good mood. Remember that we're always Ollie and Ossie when the drink wears off. And please don't aim straight, for I've got to scrub out your cabin in the morning, and wash down the deck after this wild party.'

'Silence, boy,' thundered the captain of the raiders. 'You'll call me Captain Ruff on this deck, unless you want to be thrown overboard like Griswald, who also defied my authority.'

'I'm sorry, Captain Ruff,' wept small Ossie. 'I'd hate to share the fate of Grissie, I mean Griswald. In future I'll remember my lowly place. If I *have* a future, sir!'

'Release the boy, I'm tired of this game,' scowled Olaf Ruff. Then his red face lit up in a fiendish grin. He began to bellow, 'And now, my lads, let's return to our merry-making. For with luck we'll be facing hard fighting and rich pickings in the morning. Legend tells that upstream is a valley and a hill. And coiled around that hill is a great snake made from solid gold! Our mission is to plunder every last speck of that gold and slaughter anyone who tries to stop us. And if some fools *do* try to stop us, then we'll spit them on our daggers. And should anyone dare to bleat about "How green is my valley", he'll be cleaved from head to toe by an axe. We swashbuckling northerners have no time for prissy folk who only smile when they're afraid. For only the glint and the chink of gold can make *us* smile. In short, we're here to plunder and kill, and plunder and kill we certainly will! What say you, lads?'

'With Captain Olaf Ruff as our leader, how can we fail?' yelled the crew. 'We'll be dripping with gold before this raid is through!'

'Then let's pray for the morning to come,' cried Ruff. 'Meanwhile, let's drink and dance our fill, dreaming of the moment when the prow of our ship grinds into the sands of a new shore. And what will await us there, my proud northern lads?'

'A bloody battle, we hope,' came the jubilant cry. 'And lots of giggling maidens who'll fall in love with our swashbuckling ways!'

'Well answered, my rascals,' chuckled Ruff. 'So let us make merry again. Let's enjoy ourselves before we begin our grisly work.'

And once again the anchorage came alive to the stomp of dancing feet and coarse sailors' songs. As more ale was tipped down thirsty throats, there was also the sound of clashing swords and axes, for northerners loved to fight each other when they were drunk.

Then suddenly a piercing cry was heard above the din. It was Ossie, the cabin-boy. He was pointing with a trembling finger towards a coil of rope on deck. The crew ceased their cavorting and gathered around him, grinning drunkenly. Ossie the cabin-boy was always good for a laugh.

'Something just rose from that coil of rope, then bobbed down again,' cried Ossie. 'It looked like a hairy monster with bristling whiskers. It had three heads and six eyes all glaring at me. It looked exactly like the wicked demon my grandma used to frighten me with while she fed me my milk on her lap. She always warned me that if I ever strayed from the straight and narrow the Devil would get me. And here he is in that coil of rope, getting ready to spring out at us! Please, Ollie, let's row back to our northern home before we're all turned into something nasty for a demon's tasty supper!'

'Control yourself, stupid boy,' ordered Ruff.

'The strong ale has gone to your head. And don't call me Ollie when I'm in a bad mood.'

'I can see something now,' trembled another crew member. 'The coil of rope seems to be steaming with rage in the light from the lanterns. What if Ossie's demon really is crouched inside, waiting to pounce on us?'

'Enough of this nonsense,' roared Ruff. 'Oswald, I order you to approach that coil of rope and prove yourself a fool. How can there be a demon inside an ordinary coil of rope? Get on with it, you cowardly whelp.'

'I'm approaching nothing,' said Ossie, firmly. 'I'd sooner be lashed back on the plank and have axes hurled at me.'

'Which one of you brave lads will approach that coil of rope?' said angry Ruff. 'Who'll prove to this craven cabin-boy that there's nothing to be afraid of?'

Not a soul moved. Though fearless in battle, the crew had a healthy respect for anything that smacked of magic or demons. One of the crew voiced the concerns of them all.

'Flesh and blood we'll fight, Captain Ruff,' he said. 'But not demons with three heads and six eyes that lurk in coils of rope. Like Ossie, we learned about the power of demons while burping up milk on our grandmothers' knees.'

'Why don't you go yourself?' challenged someone. 'Our clan histories tell us that the captains of raiding ships always lead from the front in times of danger.'

'And don't think I won't,' said angry Ruff. But even that fearless captain hesitated. He too had heard the same tales of terror while perched on his grandma's knee. Someone had to make a move, but who?

Meanwhile, inside the coil of rope the trio knew that the game would soon be up. Crushed together in a soaked and steaming bundle they realized that at any moment they would be unmasked as spies, and probably killed in some gruesome way. So why not reveal themselves and try to bluff things out? But in what guise, and how could they explain their presence on board the invader ship? It was Finn who came up with the desperate plan. He explained it to his anxious friends.

'The invaders are just as afraid as we are,' he whispered. 'They act fierce but their fear of demons makes children of them. Let's play on those fears while also playing for time. We'll be the demons of their nightmares. We'll boast of powers beyond their strength to fight. And if they see through us, if we should fail and lose our lives, then we'll die knowing that we tried our best to save our beloved valley.'

'For the folk of the valley I'll gladly give my life,' murmured Sage. 'As daughter of the hero Sedge, I'll face whatever comes.'

'Me too,' agreed Pansy. 'But why not take your idea further, Finn? You spoke of finding a chink in the armour of the invaders. Well, I think we've already met that chink, in the scruffy person of the wizard of The Briars, namely Berrybottom. If we claimed to be his assistants and protected by his magical powers, then these ruffians would think twice about using us for axe-throwing practice.'

'But Berrybottom's a fraud,' said Finn, bewildered. 'Everyone knows that.'

'Captain Olaf Ruff and his crew don't,' said Pansy. 'And we're not about to tell them. What do you think?'

'It could work,' murmured Finn. 'I always knew that you were more than just a silly hat. We'll play your game of bluff.'

'A wise decision, Finn,' grinned Pansy. 'I always knew that you were more than just an idle fisherman resting on past laurels!'

'So let's get to it,' said Sage, impatiently, 'and play our parts to the best of our ability . . .'

It was probably coincidence, but as the trio rose from the coil of rope a bolt of lightning flashed across the sky. It was followed by a roll of growling thunder. Then it began to rain in huge and spattering drops as dark clouds filled the sky. But, just as quickly, they scudded away before the wind, revealing the moonlit and starry sky once more.

That chance event had thoroughly alarmed the superstitious invaders. Their fears were stoked even more violently when the demon within the coil of rope suddenly rose and stood revealed. Just as Ossie had said, it had three heads and six eyes and was also festooned with strands of slimy green weed. For a while it just hulked and stared, its huge misshapen body gently steaming in the light from the lanterns. Then suddenly, in a quick and sinister way it divided into three parts. One of the parts advanced and spoke to the cringing sailors.

'Who is your leader?' it snapped. 'I am Finn, one of the many pairs of eyes of the great wizard Berrybottom of The Briars. My angry master demands to know why you trespass in his magical valley without permission. Be warned, beware the wrath of Berrybottom if your excuse is feeble and falls on his deaf ears.'

'He's talking to you, Ollie,' hissed Ossie,

pushing the captain to the fore. 'Be brave for us. Take all the blame on yourself as a good leader should. We'll be backing you up from behind.'

'I am Olaf Ruff, captain of this ship,' said Ruff, trying to hide his fear. His mind was working furiously to think of a good excuse. Then it came to him in a cunning flash. 'Our reason for sailing into this part of the world is a peaceful one. The lads behind me belong to The Lovers of Nature Society. They chartered my ship to explore the beauty of this valley. Some collect plants, some are bird-watchers, and others paint scenic landscapes. We come in total peace, I assure you.'

'Oh, please believe him,' prayed Ossie under his breath. The crew all had their fingers crossed behind their backs, hoping that Ruff's tall story would work. It did not.

'If you come in peace, then why do you glitter with armour and axes?' said Finn, sternly. 'Your excuse isn't good enough, Captain Ruff.'

Ossie groaned, while the crew shrank closer together. Their hearts sank even lower as the second part of the demon from the coil of rope approached them. For it was clearly a girl, and girls in their northern world always confined themselves to gutting fish and raising fierce sons.

'I am called Pansy,' she said, glaring at the cringing crew from beneath her sodden hat. Then she pointed a warning finger at the sky. 'I advise you to tell the truth before the wizard Berrybottom strikes this ship with a thunderbolt, and drowns you all. Or he might in his angry fury turn you all into hopping toads. He could even vanish you all completely, if he chose. For such is his power when annoyed. Even now our master is watching you through our six eyes, weighing your lies. So I strongly urge you to turn this ship around and row back to the northlands as fast as you can. The choice is yours, Captain Olaf Ruff. But I hope that you make the right decision for all of your sakes, for the wrong choice spells misery and death.'

'Grovel for us, Ollie,' pleaded Ossie. 'We're in a no-win situation here. These demons know that we haven't come here to link daisy chains. I don't want to drown, and I don't want to be a hopping toad, and I don't want to be vanished for ever when I've only just started to live. Please do the sensible thing, my captain! Let's make a dash for our oars and put plenty of clear blue water between us and this spooky valley.'

But for all his bullying and bluster, Ruff was not a complete coward. He was also smart, in a devious way, which was why he had risen through the ranks from cabin-boy to become the captain of a raiding ship. But his ambition reached much higher. He was determined to prove his worth by arriving back in the northlands with the largest haul of gold his people had ever gaped at. So he decided to play for time, to find out more about this Berrybottom of so-called magical powers.

Now there were two sides intent on playing for time. When the third part of Ossie's demon padded forward to speak, Ruff noted that it was a furry water creature and a female one at that. Ruff was becoming less impressed and more suspicious with every passing moment. He still remained cautious, though inwardly fuming as the vole shook muddy water all over him.

'My name is Sage,' she said quietly. 'And I can only echo the words of my friends. I urge you and your crew to turn and row away before something terrible befalls you. I urge you to heed our warning, for the anger of Berrybottom cannot be contained once unleashed.'

'I'm heeding and I'm also doubting, muddy vole,' sneered Ruff. 'For me, your gang of three just doesn't ring true. My simple-minded crew might have imagined a trio of demons rising from a coil of rope, but I wasn't so easily fooled. I just saw two phonies and a rat, and a smelly one at that. So I challenge you to demonstrate the power of your Berrybottom master. I offer as his first victim my ship's cabin-boy. Conjure up this wizard and tell him to turn the boy into a toad – if he can. Then perhaps we might believe your wild claims.'

'Why pick on me, Ollie?' cried Ossie. 'All I've

ever done is sweep the decks and tidy your cabin after your drunken rages. Now I'm going to end up as an ugly toad through no fault of my own. My grandma warned me not to go to sea. I should have stayed close to her knee and listened more.'

'Control yourself, you stupid boy,' snapped Ruff. Then he smiled triumphantly at the trio. 'So, what happened to the magical powers of your great wizard Berrybottom? My cabin-boy is still a cabin-boy, and certainly not a toad.'

'Our master can sometimes be merciful,' lied Finn. 'He must have spared your cabin-boy for his own mysterious reasons.'

'I'd like to meet this Berrybottom,' said Ruff, abruptly. Now he was calling their bluff. 'When can it be arranged? I'd like to meet him face to face and speak about our peaceful intentions. Where can he be found?'

'He's climbing a hill on business at the moment,' said Finn, quickly. 'We don't know when he plans to climb down again, though.'

'He might never climb down at all,' said Pansy.

'One never knows with the wizard of The Briars. He might even decide to climb halfway up and stay there.'

'And weave his powerful magic halfway up, and halfway down the hill,' nodded Sage. 'For any place can serve as a stage for Berrybottom to weave his power. And who can understand how the mind of a genius wizard works?'

'You can't, and that's a fact,' sneered Ruff. 'Even my cabin-boy can read my mind, can't you, boy?'

'Yes, Ollie,' babbled Ossie. 'I can read your mind before a thought enters it. Staying one step ahead of your thoughts has kept me alive so far.'

'So,' said Ruff, evilly eyeing the nervous trio. 'Until your master demonstrates his powers you'll be treated as illegal stowaways. Which means making yourselves useful. The use I have in mind is to perform a task while my lusty lads and I wait for the sun to rise.'

'What task would that be?' asked Finn, his heart sinking.

'Targets for our practice,' said brutal Ruff. 'The

axes of my crew must find their mark when we do battle in the morning. They need to hone their skill in readiness, so as to be perfect when the moment comes. Your lives will depend on keeping still while they attempt to clip your ears, without causing too much damage. Lads, seize the stowaways and lash them to the practice-plank. And I'm offering an extra share of gold to the warrior who parts that silly hat from the girl's head, for it irritates me very much.'

The crew, suddenly brave again, grinningly carried out his orders. The relief they felt expressed itself in violence. Their fears of thunderbolts and being turned into toads was behind them. Ruff was now in charge again, and all was well on the ship.

Seizing the terrified friends they frog-marched them to the dreaded plank. Binding them fast, they took ten paces back and tested their axes for sharpness. Then, one by one, they toed the line and hurled their deadly missiles, trying to miss their trembling targets as closely as possible. One or two whistling axes went astray. Sage whimpered softly as an errant throw sliced through the tip of her ear, causing blood to flow. Finn gasped in pain as the wooden haft of one clumsily thrown weapon struck his forehead, leaving an ugly wound. The most cheered throw pinned Pansy's hat and a clump of her hair to the plank. But she refused to show distress, much to the anger of the gloating Ruff.

Then tiring of the game, the crew began to drink and sing once again, stumbling around and arguing amongst themselves. But soon they felt the need to sleep. One by one they slumped to the deck, and began to snore and dream. But dream of what? A single voice cried out in sleep for a faraway loved one, for some childish comfort long left behind. Then it faded away to be lost in the babble and groans of a host of lonely sailors far from home. They had chosen their beds and there they lay, waiting for the sun to rise to warm their chilled bodies and souls.

Through those early hours the three pinioned

friends whispered encouragement to each other, hoping that the new day would bring them help. Now and again they would drift off into a fitful sleep, their pains soothed for a while by the hope of rescue . . . Meanwhile, some hours before . . .

Nine

OUR FRIENDS ON THE HILL

Two figures dressed in golden snakeskin stood on the top of Buttercup Hill and watched the small party toiling upwards. Lit by moonlight, the figures soon became familiar. Moments later Umber and Amber of the Guardian Clan were delightedly greeting their old friends from the valley below. For the Guardians of the Great

Golden Snake, a visit from the Willow Clan was always welcome, day or night. As well as exchanging gossip, the Guardians were eager to tell their visitors how busy their clan had been since the great snake had curled up and gone to sleep for one hundred years. Neither Umber nor Amber noticed the worry on the faces of Nettles and Poppy as they babbled out their latest news . . .

'The building of Snakehenge is progressing well,' said Umber, proudly. 'After only one year into his long sleep our snake is almost completely ringed around with giant stones. The henge will be a fitting monument to him when he awakens. Oh, what a celebration that will be for our grandchildren to witness.'

'Even the most distant guardian groups heeded our call,' enthused Amber. 'When they learned that our Snake was at peace with his tail and had gone to sleep, they all set to with a will. So you see, we Guardians are still tending our golden friend even while he slumbers and dreams. Our youngsters needed some cajoling at first but they soon fell in with the task when we explained the importance of it. We still get the odd childish grumble, but you know how the young are . . .'

'But we're talking too much!' cried Umber. 'You don't know how pleased we are to see you. And you're just in time to enjoy a late supper.'

Soon everyone was sitting around a glowing fire enjoying a meal of silverfish baked in honey, plus warming bowls of mead that made the senses reel a mite. Yet throughout that pleasant starlit meal it became obvious to Umber and Amber that something was troubling Nettles. When they learned that the kitchen-boy was now leader of the Willow Clan they were surprised, but not too much. On the quest to the end of the tail he had always shown promise. But they did feel sympathy for him, for leadership always entails worries as they both well knew. So, politely, they curbed their curiosity and waited for the boy to unburden himself in his own good time.

In the meantime they were gazing in fascination

at the strange person who sat amongst their visitors. As well as stuffing down most of the silverfish and swigging the free mead, he kept scratching himself in a very off-putting way. They also noticed that he kept staring at the head of their Great Golden Snake with a greedy, lustful gaze. Questions needed to be asked.

'Excuse me, Nettles, but you haven't introduced your friend,' said Umber, politely. 'Who is he, we wonder? A friend of yours, of course.'

'A friend who honours us with his hearty appetite,' Amber hastened to say. 'But does he have a skin problem by any chance? Perhaps we could help in some way.'

'His name is Berrybottom of The Briars and he claims to be a wizard,' said angry Nettles. 'And why he's got an irritable skin we don't know, or care. But he certainly irritates us. We try to ignore him, and suggest that you do too. And he's not remotely a friend of ours, even though he'd like to be.'

'He's demanding three sacks of gold from us,'

explained Poppy. 'For services he claims he rendered, but didn't. That's why he's followed us here. Berrybottom refuses to go away until he's been paid in full.'

Berrybottom nodded and grinned and stuffed more fish in his mouth.

'But it's best not to provoke him,' said Meadowsweet, quickly. 'Because being a wizard he could turn us into toads if he lost his temper.'

'He might even turn me into a prince,' smiled Teasel. 'The handsome prince that you've been waiting for.'

'And I'd still tell you to hop off,' snapped Meadowsweet.

'Are you sure he doesn't have magical powers?' asked Amber, frowning as Berrybottom flashed her a broad wink.

'Sensible folk doubt it,' said Poppy. 'Only silly people believe a word that Berrybottom says. Nettles and I are determined to keep him at a sensible arm's-length distance from our friendship.'

'I'm not surprised that he's a fraud,' agreed Amber. 'A real wizard would surely keep himself free from fleas with a quick magic potion.'

'Nettles,' said Umber, butting in. 'Isn't it time that you told us about the real problem that worries you? Let we Guardians share it. Isn't that what you came here for?'

And so Nettles launched into the story about the invader ship approaching the valley and the threat it posed to their peaceful way of life. He told about the wasted voyage to buy some wise advice from Berrybottom, only to find out that it was worthless and vastly overpriced. He ended by saying that the so-called wizard of The Briars was not only a fool, but greedy too, and that his clinging presence was only adding to the problems the Willow Clan faced. Having heard not one good word said about him, Berrybottom's grin faded and he began to scratch himself even more.

'There's nothing wrong with Berrybottom that a happy life won't cure,' said Meadowsweet, defending him. 'His problem is Crabapple who nags him all the time. She's the greedy one, with her grasping for gold.'

'How about the three wives before her?' argued Teasel. 'They also nagged him and made his life a misery. So his problem is that he constantly chooses the wrong partners to marry!'

'Which I'd have no problem with,' snapped Meadowsweet. 'Especially if that wrong partner was sitting much too close to me and talking in my ear.'

'But you listen,' grinned Teasel.

'So, Umber and Amber, it all comes down to this,' said Nettles. 'We're here to ask for your help. For we've no one else to turn to in our ebbing hours of need.'

'When did you first spy this incoming ship?' asked Umber, concerned.

'I didn't spy it myself,' admitted Nettles. 'But I know someone who did.'

'It's about time I was mentioned,' cried fuming Jenny. 'I noticed that you introduced Berrybottom quickly enough. Yet I'm the only one who's actually seen the shipful of fierce warriors all thirsting for your blood!'

'How could I forget?' sighed Nettles. 'Umber, Amber, the tiny bird you see perched on the nose of your giant snake is Jenny wren, our new scout.'

'And also your personal companion for life,' added Jenny, fluffing her feathers importantly. 'You and Poppy would still be kitchen-slaves if it wasn't for me.'

'Poor Nettles,' said Umber, feelingly. 'To have so many problems this early in your life must be a weighty burden. First of all an invading ship, then a dubious wizard with a lust for gold, plus a cheeky bird with a taste for power. I'm amazed that you took on the leadership of your clan at all. Frankly, if I were in your position I'd be tempted to throw up my hands and run away as fast as I could.'

'Umber wouldn't really run away,' assured Amber. 'He's stronger than he knows. His is a quiet and modest strength that endures through thick and thin. He's quite aware that the foreign ship is as much a danger to us as to you Willow folk. He'd never desert his friends and flee like a coward. He swears this on the sacred nose of our Great Golden Snake. Don't you, Umber?'

'Of course,' said Umber, hastily. 'That's what I meant to say. I was just posing the question of what a coward would do if he were me.'

'Having never been a coward yourself,' said Amber, watching him closely. 'Choose your words carefully before you answer.'

'My words are chosen and now I'll speak them!' cried Umber, leaping to his feet. In a ringing voice he addressed his clan who were squatting around their fires and munching baked silverfish.

'My people, as the leader of the Buttercup Hill Guardians I've decided to join forces with Nettles and the Willow Clan. The invading ship now approaching our valley is a threat to the lives of us all. Nettles plans to fight the barbarians on the beach as they wade ashore. And we, my brave Guardian warriors, will be brawling on the sands beside him. What say you, my valiant friends?'

A throaty roar of approval rose from around the flickering fires.

'This could prove to be our finest hour,' yelled Amber, striding amongst the fires. 'We may be chopped to bits by the sharp axes of the enemy, but we Guardians will never be enslaved!'

'What are we waiting for, Nettles?' shouted Umber. 'We Guardians are ready to march down the hill under your command!'

'I think we should first check on Berrybottom,' said Poppy, uneasily. 'While you were declaring war I noticed him slipping away. And being on the loose, his charm could be spreading amongst your older ladies. For it's no secret that he's looking for a new wife to replace the nagging Crabapple. I'm thinking he could cause a rash of jealousy to break out around your fires.'

After a frantic search, Berrybottom was found, or rather surprised. He was crouched under the head of the great snake busily stuffing flakes of golden skin into one of his sacks. He showed no guilt at all when he was ordered to creep out. Instead he looked disappointed.

'Gold should come in heavy lumps,' he complained. 'This stuff is as light as feathers. A real sackful should make me sweat to drag it. The three sackfuls I'm owed should make me burst a rupture just to budge it. I hope you're not fobbing me off with fools' gold. Because Crabapple will throw a fit when she finds out. Though I've grown to like you very much, I'll still turn you all into toads or vanish you for ever if you go back on our bargain.'

'Your threats are wearing thin, Berrybottom,' warned Nettles.

'And so is our patience,' snapped Poppy. 'How dare you show us up before our friends with your gorging and flirting and stealing.'

'I'm afraid the only fool is you, wizard Berrybottom,' sighed Amber. 'Our great snake is not made of real gold at all. He's just the colour of gold, which is completely different.'

'So why not go home to The Briars and to

Crabapple?' pleaded Nettles. 'And leave we band of friends to get on with saving our valley?'

'I'll never go home while Crabapple is there,' shuddered Berrybottom, scratching himself vigorously again. 'At least, not without three sacks of gold. I should have sent her into limbo on our wedding day because of her nagging. But I hadn't enough ingredients in my pouch. Anyway, she would only have joined my other wives who taunt me from the trees. So I've decided to divorce her from a distance and find a new wife. One who won't nag me from dawn till dusk.'

'A vain hope,' said Poppy, shaking her head. 'Looking at you, I think that you're the kind of husband that needs to be nagged. I'd sympathize with any wife who had to put up with your disgusting scratching and your unkempt appearance. I suggest that you scrub yourself down and start afresh. And if you want to divorce Crabapple, then you should tell her to her face. That's the honourable thing to do.'

'You've witnessed her temper,' winced Berrybottom, his grubby nails clawing at his neck. 'How could I take home wife number five with Crabapple still ruling the roost? I'd prefer to stay here where I'm safe, with all my new friends, who've shown me what happiness is.'

'We've heard enough of Berrybottom's self-pity,' said Nettles, impatiently. 'Let him pull his own hot chestnuts out of the fire. Not once has he shown concern for the saving of our valley from the invaders. All he cares about is his own selfish self and nuggets of gold.'

'And pretty ladies!' leered Berrybottom, winking at outraged Amber. Then he grimaced and began to scratch his armpit. To the worry of Umber and Amber a few young Guardians began to giggle and scratch in imitation. It was clear they were admiring and copying his horrible habit. In fact, they had never met such a charming rascal. They didn't care that he had scoffed most of their silverfish supper and had stolen a sack of dandruff from their great snake. Some of the ladies were so smitten that they were even making eyes at him. Realizing that he was losing control, Umber rose, stood in the light from the flickering fires, and addressed them again in urgent tones.

'My family, step forward the brave ones prepared to give their lives in defence of Buttercup Hill and our Great Golden Snake. Those of you who stay behind must continue the building of Snakehenge, the monument to our sleeping friend and hero, for it must be completed.'

'Proudly built in everlasting stone,' cried Amber, weeping. 'And also in honour of we fighters who may never return to adore our great snake again.'

'Let not this spear sleep in my hand,' vowed a valiant youngster, 'till we have built our Snakehenge in this green and buttercupped land.'

'Lead us down into the heat of battle, Umber,' yelled a voice. 'As for our coming back up again, we'll shift for ourselves!'

Umber's call to arms was quickly answered.

Those eager to fight had risen from their firesides to rally around him. They looked impressive in their gold snakeskin tunics and caps, brandishing the barbed tridents that they used for spearing silverfish.

And so, to lusty cheers from the stay-at-homes, the enlarged party of Nettles, Poppy, Umber and Amber wended down the hill in single file to the valley below, to face whatever they must. Scrambling along behind came Berrybottom hugging his few possessions and his sack of gold flakings, pausing to scratch his itchy spots at every opportunity. He was certainly getting around these days, was the wizard of The Briars. And he was enjoying it very much. If this was happiness then he wanted more – in fact, his lust for contentment was replacing his lust for gold. Then suddenly his joy turned to fear, for as he bowled along in the wake of the others he heard a familiar and blood-chilling chant coming from a clump of bushes . . .

'Hurry, scurry, Berrybottom,
Fleeing from your wicked past,
We your wives will end your story,
That we might find peace at last.'

They were the taunting voices of Nightshade, Leafmould and Sourseed, the wives he had spelled into the limbo-world of neither here nor there. They had followed his flight from The Briars and were now lying in wait to remind him that his fate was hanging by a thread, if they had anything to do with it. The gruesome smell from their bubbling pot struck terror into Berrybottom's heart. He knew that smell full well. It told him that his vengeful wives were getting close to solving the vanishing spell that had defeated his forebears for so long. The spell that had frustrated him for the whole of his life. It had always been so near, yet so far. Just that one vital ingredient was all that was needed. But what was it, and where could it be found? And what if his hate-filled wives discovered the vital secret before he did? It would mean that the great wizard, Berrybottom of The Briars, would be vanished from existence just as he was learning what true happiness was! And that would be intolerable.

With rising panic in his breast he hurried on, the cackling voices pursuing him . . .

'Tremble through your nights, false husband . . . count them as they slip away . . . soon cold death will tap your shoulder . . . then the dark will claim your day . . .'

'Tremble through your own ghostly nights,' yelled Berrybottom, dashing past the bushes. 'My nose is on the brink of a vital discovery, don't you worry. And when I do crack the secret of the spell *I'll* be doing the vanishing around this valley. And the first ones to go will be you three nagging hags!'

And with their harsh laughter still ringing in his ears he hurried to catch up with his new friends, looking constantly over his shoulder as he thankfully left the clump of bushes far behind . . .

Ten

'TREACHERY!' CAME THE CRY

With the dawn so near to breaking, Nettles had planned to march straight down to the stream, to resist the invaders on the beach when they tried to land. So he was annoyed to be hailed by a lookout perched high in the branches of the home oak. The lookout, shouting something about 'foul treachery', could well ruin the plans of the new leader.

'Your presence is needed immediately,' cried the lookout, before ducking back behind a thick curtain of leaves.

Glancing worriedly at the brightening sky, Nettles the leader needed to make a decision. Treachery could spell his downfall, but so could the invasion if his forces were not in place to meet it. He decided that he urgently needed to know what had happened in the oak while he had been away. Halting the fired-up warriors, he told them that the plan had been changed, saying that they would settle the treachery problem first, which was probably a fuss about nothing anyway. He sought to soothe their grumblings with a joke.

'After all, we had a late supper, why not an early breakfast?' he grinned. 'And the sun won't rise until it's ready to, so why try to steal a march on it? And we all know how sluggishly it rises some mornings. Perhaps the invaders are also lazy and prone to lateness so early in the day. In the meantime we'll post sentries to keep watch on the stream. They'll soon warn us if the ship sails in earlier than expected . . .' But his excuses sounded very uncertain and lame in the circumstances.

Nettles ignored the applause as he and his small army trooped into the meeting hall. Anyway, he sensed that the clapping was prompted by fear, rather than the warmth of greeting. Then very quickly, a worried silence descended around the packed hall. It was clear the urgent message from the lookout had not been an idle one. Something serious had happened while Nettles and his friends had been away. It was Robin, an old leader of yesteryear, who told Nettles the bad news.

'I'm afraid I must tell you that Finn and Pansy and Sage have deserted to the enemy,' he said, still in a state of shock. 'The moment you left the three of them were seen whispering together. Then they suddenly slipped from this hall without a word to anyone. They were soon spotted heading downstream by a lookout, swimming in the direction of the ship. I hate to accuse, but I sense treachery, Nettles.'

'Terrible treachery from the treasured trio we

trusted,' grieved his partner, Fern. 'I wouldn't believe it, were it not so.'

'We don't believe that Finn and Pansy would betray us,' cried some folk from the audience. 'And neither would our steadfast Sage.'

'Old Sedge the vole would collapse to hear such news,' cried someone. 'Which is why Sage his daughter would never dishonour him so. I refuse to believe this rumour of treachery.'

'And so do many more of us,' came the defiant shout.

'It's true that the treachery of the trio is yet to be proved,' admitted Nettles. 'But we can't afford to take chances. For the sake of the valley they must be considered guilty of whispering our plans to the enemy. For why else would they sneak off downstream?'

'Even I hope that Pansy is innocent,' said Poppy. 'I'd hate to think of her carousing on board the enemy ship in that ridiculous hat, and being cheered and toasted by that ruffian crew.'

'So, my decision is that Finn and Pansy and

Sage are guilty until proved innocent,' said Nettles, sadly. 'Yet it's too late to alter my plan if they have betrayed it. We must hope for the best and press on. What else can we do?'

'I know what else you can do,' cried a familiar voice. 'You can all get a good, filling breakfast inside you before you start this battling nonsense.'

It was Granny Willow. She came bustling into the meeting hall, her steaming spoon smelling of delicious things. She smiled triumphantly at Nettles. 'I knew you'd soon come dashing back for a bowl of my stew. And so, into the dining hall with you all. We'll soon have those worried frowns chased away by the smiles of full bellies. For as I've always said, problems are caused by lack of regular meals.'

Most everyone agreed that Granny Willow was right. Soon the Willow folk and their Guardian friends were crowding in to breakfast. Though he had arrived late because of waylaying wives, Berrybottom beat the swiftest of runners to the table, tucking a gold sack into his tunic to serve as a bib. Then Granny Willow came hobbling into the hall, her plump face dripping sweat. Behind her staggered Rosie and Thorn bearing a huge cauldron of stew between them. Balanced on their heads were piles of sparkling clean stew bowls. Though hating their work as kitchen-slaves they were grinning and bearing it, for they were certain that they had their feet on the first ladder-rung to fame and fortune, just like lucky Nettles and Poppy.

Granny Willow watched proudly as everyone tucked in. She was extra pleased with Berrybottom who gobbled and gasped through several helpings, greedily mopping up the juices with hunks of acorn bread. Finally, Nettles, who had refused to eat a scrap, could stand no more. He had been watching the rays of the early sun streaming in through the rough-hewn windows of the oak. Getting to his feet, he impatiently brandished his sword above his head.

'What kind of warriors are we?' he cried, 'who sit enjoying breakfast while our enemies bear down upon us? We should be down on the beach, preparing to do or die. For see, already the sun is up.'

'And the morning has broken,' chimed in Poppy. 'Do we need the early blackbirds to remind us?'

'We'll be our own early birds,' shouted the Willow warriors, rising as one. 'Lead on down to the beach, Nettles. And if we should taste defeat, let this breakfast be our last repast.'

'My fighters are also ready, Nettles,' cried Umber. 'We're ready to march, just say the word.'

'Well, Berrybottom isn't ready to march,' snapped Granny Willow. 'His digestion is more important than playing at warriors. He's still slurping the last dregs from my stew cauldron, and enjoying every slurp. And he's also asked me to marry him when he's freed himself from Crabapple.'

But the last thing on Nettles' mind was Berrybottom's romantic life and stomach. He was soon forming the warriors into ranks at the foot of the oak for the march down to the beach. Before moving off he spoke a few encouraging words to them, to steel their hearts, as well as his own. Then with his mind seething with doubts and worries about what the treacherous trio might have told the enemy, he led them away. Now he truly had to prove himself a worthy leader. He was determined to do so. He would save the valley from the invaders, even if it cost him his life.

The unpleasant meeting with his ex-wives forgotten, Berrybottom was cheerful as he followed behind the warriors, burping heartily after his huge breakfast. If he heard the sinister cackling and the scuffling in the bushes, he gave no sign, for he blotted all nasty things from his mind. He had a new and happy life and he was hanging on to it. His ghostly wives could make all the threats they wished and he would ignore them. Hugging his spell-pot and gold sacks he scurried along on his bandy legs in the wake of the war party.

Arriving at the beach, he mingled happily amongst his new friends. He seemed not to notice their tension and fear as they assembled to face the stream. But then the wizard of The Briars had never cared about the problems of others. Being totally selfish he believed that the only problems on earth were his own. His personal happiness was the only thing that mattered to him – the happiness of others concerned him not a jot. That was the way Berrybottom's mind worked. It had been the way of every Berrybottom down the ages. And it sadly seemed that it always would be so.

Not too far away strutted another like-minded soul, a tiny bird so swelled with self-importance that, if she wasn't careful, she would self-destruct in a puff of unlamented feathers one day . . .

Eleven

JENNY STRUTS HER STUFF

So fraught had been the events of the morning, that no one had noticed the absence of Jenny wren. None had realized that her piping voice had been missing during the breakfast break at the oak. In fact, that mischievous bird had her own plans for the dawning morning. She had vowed to be the close companion of Nettles for life. But

Jenny had always been her own closest companion and friend. Since hatching from her egg, she had set out to be a lone, free-flying little liar, and she gloried in it. Her lifestyle was to use others to satisfy her boundless curiosity, only to discard them when they began to bore her. She was proud of her smooth and flattering tongue that could make folk believe whatever she wished them to. Hadn't she only recently raised a lowly kitchen-boy to become leader of his clan?

But what Jenny gave she also took away, when the petulant whim moved her. She would happily destroy with lies the ones who had come to trust her. That was the reason why she had winged downstream that early morning, without telling a soul. She was itching with curiosity to take a closer look at the bristling ship and its crew. For excitement was her craving, variety was her need. And restlessly she sought it . . .

Perching on a coil of rope, Jenny's beady eyes took in the scene. All her romantic notions vanished. Where was the sound of jolly Jack Tars chanting sea-shanties as they heaved on ropes to prepare the vessel for sailing? Had she come to the wrong ship? she grinned, mockingly. Her tidy mind was appalled as she glanced around at the drunken sailors slumped on the deck, groaning in their nightmares. Weapons littered the planking and empty ale-barrels rolled from port to starboard, as the ship heaved in the gentle swell of the harbour. At the stern the rudder swung listlessly free for want of a sober seaman to lash it down. The oars of the raiding ship no longer bristled but were as tangled as a log-jam. Whoever the captain of this vessel was should be thoroughly ashamed, mused disgusted Jenny. As there was not a single soul awake she pursed her beak and uttered a few shrill whistles.

'Ahoy there, captain,' she called. 'As there's no one on watch I've piped myself aboard. To use a nautical term, would you mind showing a leg, please?'

The reply was just more moans and groans. Then the bird began to hear faint voices. Curious, she looked around. Then to her astonishment she saw, lashed to a plank of wood, three figures she knew very well.

'Help us, Jenny wren,' murmured Finn, his face bloody, his dull eyes pleading.

'Oh, the relief to see a friendly face,' wept Pansy, her hat scalped from her head by an expert axe-throw.

'Rescue at last,' sighed Sage. 'A thousand welcomes, little bird.'

'Deary me, what a sad sight,' mocked Jenny, relishing the moment. 'The three traitors reduced to grovelling for help. I think I should warn you that my master Nettles has condemned you all to death for consorting with the enemy. So I'm afraid I can't help you at all. Anyway, my beak is for talking, not for gnawing through ropes.'

'Why do you call us traitors?' asked Finn, bewildered.

'Everyone is doing so back at the oak,' smirked Jenny. 'Your names are now greeted by hisses and curses. Everyone agrees that you fled here to throw in your lot with the invaders to save your miserable skins. But obviously your treacherous plan came unstuck. The invaders must have decided that you were double agents. For why else would you be tied to that plank, bitten by axe-marks, and bleeding to boot?'

'But we came here to trick the invaders,' said desperate Finn. 'We hoped that the name of Berrybottom, wizard of The Briars would strike fear into their hearts and make them row away from our valley.'

'We hoped to find a chink in their armour, you see,' whispered Pansy. 'And we thought we had found it. We discovered that the invaders become childish with terror when the words "magic" or "demons" are mentioned. So we thought to frighten them with the name of Berrybottom and his powers.'

'But of course, it didn't work,' giggled Jenny. 'Lying is an art, you see. The success of a lie is to make an untruth believable. But of course I'm speaking to novices who've stupidly lied themselves into a corner, with no fib out.'

'Our undercover plan could still work, Jenny,' pleaded Sage. 'If you would back up our Berrybottom story.'

'If your expert lies could truly terrify Captain Olaf Ruff and his crew,' agreed Finn.

'You could warn them that Berrybottom is pacing about in a terrible rage,' said Pansy eagerly. 'With bolts of lightning flashing from his fingertips, and with his awesome face as black as thunder.'

'But Berrybottom's a fraud, we all know that,' grinned Jenny. 'The last time I saw him he was filling his belly with silverfish and stuffing fools' gold into a sack. And all with a stupid grin on his ugly face.'

'At least you could try, Jenny,' pleaded Finn. 'Even if only to gain a bit more time for our family to prepare their defences.'

'I'll think about it,' teased the bird.

Just then a voice was heard coming nearer, a despairing and grumbling voice. It was Ossie the cabin-boy, up early as usual and complaining about all the rubbish and chaos everywhere. He began to sweep between and around the drunken bodies with a twig broom, muttering all the time . . .

'And who has to clean up after their drunken bouts? Ossie does. And who never receives one word of thanks? Ossie. Who wishes he never went to sea and stayed near his grandma's knee? Ossie. And who's going to jump overboard and become a landlubber if he isn't treated better? Ossie isn't, because he's too frightened of Ollie. And who is the little bird who keeps staring at me, spying on my sweeping? Ossie doesn't know. So who are you, little bird, and what do you want?'

For a while there was silence. Finn and Pansy and Sage were gazing pleadingly at Jenny, who had hopped from the coil of rope to the top of the torture plank. Then the bird made up her devious mind. To the relief of the imprisoned trio she decided to play the game their way, for the while. Fluffing up her feathers and standing on tiptoe she addressed the frightened cabin-boy.

'I've been sent here by the all-powerful Berrybottom,' she shrilled, 'who demands that you obey his every command. Go and rouse the captain of this ship before something awful befalls you all. Go and tell him that Jenny, Berrybottom's right-hand bird, awaits his humble presence on deck. Go . . . quickly now, gaping boy!'

'Yes, Miss Jenny,' babbled Ossie, dropping his broom. 'I'll rush and shake Ollie awake at once. And if things get nasty later on, please remember that I'm only a cabin-boy who was forced to go to sea against his will. The salty waves were never in my blood, you see . . .' and he hared off down to the captain's cabin.

'A Miss Jenny Bird said what?' roared a voice from below. 'Nobody shakes me from my own bunk on my own ship. And certainly not with threats. I don't care who she says she is. Where's my breeches and my war-axe, you little wretch?'

Moments later Ruff came storming on deck, cursing and kicking the drunken crew to their feet.

Then his bleary eyes focussed on Jenny. He glared. She returned his challenging glare with one of her own. For a while they glared at each other, clearly engaged in a battle of wills. Who would blink first?

It was Ruff who did, as his eyes began to water. Realizing she was the winner, Jenny remained cool and collected as she began to take him to task. For such a tiny bird she was extremely confident as she pressed her advantage. Not even the war-axe gleaming on Ruff's shoulder seemed to worry her.

'Don't fidget when I'm speaking to you,' she snapped. 'And if that sounds like a threat it's because it is. First of all, don't even dream about laying one grubby finger on me because I'm under the protection of Berrybottom of The Briars, the most powerful wizard in the valley of the People. In fact his spells and potions are so strong that they make even my cool head spin. So think deeply, Captain Olaf Ruff. I'm now ordering you to release your prisoners from that torture plank.

They are just harmless and humble servants of Berrybottom who foolishly got above themselves. I, my master's right-hand bird am taking charge to sort this nonsense out. Next I demand that you get this ship underway at once. You will sail it upstream to where Berrybottom is pacing the beach, his face purple with rage that you should dare enter his valley without permission!'

'And if I refuse?' snarled Ruff. 'These prisoners also made threats, and look at them now. You could also be bluffing, Miss Jenny Smartbeak.'

At his words Jenny appeared to go into a deep trance. Her tiny body swayed and her beady eyes took on a glazed look. But for her claws embedded in the plank she would have toppled from her perch, so out-of-body did she seem to be. Then suddenly she began to speak in a strange and harsh voice. The words that came from her beak were so frightening that the crew, and even Ruff, shrank back in dread.

'I am the mighty wizard Berrybottom,' rasped a deep voice that sounded weird to be coming from such a small throat. 'When you question the word of my right-hand Jenny, you question mine. Be warned, invaders of my valley, obey her commands or answer to me. I order you to sail into my presence, to answer to the crime of imprisoning my humble servants. Failure to do so will result in your suffering many unpleasant fates. Some I will turn into toads, others like Captain Olaf Ruff I'll vanish completely from the face of the earth for ever. Doubt my powers at your peril. Bow your heads to Jenny bird or prepare to meet your doom.'

'There's that toad threat again,' sobbed Ossie. 'Please, Ollie, I don't want to be an ugly toad. Obey Miss Jenny before I'm forced to jump overboard and vanish myself without magic.'

'Where am I?' asked Jenny, shaking her head in bewilderment. 'I feel like I've been in a trance. And my throat is so sore and dry, though I don't know why.'

'It's because the wizard Berrybottom has been speaking through you,' yelled Ossie. 'And he's threatened to turn me into a toad again. Please, Ollie, I don't know how much more of this tension my nerves will stand!'

'Release the prisoners,' ordered Ruff, also badly shaken but masking his fear. 'Then prepare to get underway. Break out the oars and bend to them. Together we'll face this Berrybottom of The Briars. Perhaps he really does have magical powers we can't fight. If so, we can always find another valley to invade. But there's always the chance that everything is one huge bluff. In which case we'll ravage and devastate this valley with every fibre of fury we possess. One thing is certain, one way or another we'll return to the northlands with a ship filled with gold to be hailed as heroes. What do you say, my lusty lads?'

'We say aye, aye, Captain Ruff,' roared the crew, springing to carry out his orders.

'Notice I didn't shout "Aye, aye," ' cried Ossie. 'Please make a kindly note of that, Miss Jenny Bird. I never ever got my sea-legs. Perhaps mighty Berrybottom could find me a shore job?'

170

But no one was listening to the terrified cabin-boy who was bitterly wishing he had stayed at home, close to his grandmother's knee.

And so the bristling ship sailed out into the main stream, oars flashing, the rudderman heaving as he steered the vessel upstream against the rapids. While the released trio of Finn, Pansy and Sage tended to each other's wounds and anguished about the outcome of this nightmare voyage, Jenny was perched on the prow of the ship, her feathers fluttering in the wind, enjoying herself enormously.

What better thrill than that of power, she mused to herself. With so many in my thrall, and me so small and all . . .

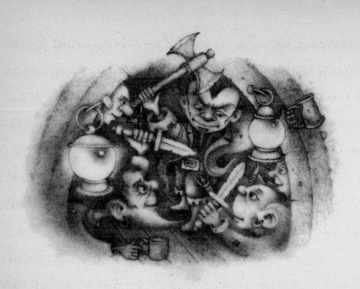

Twelve

A Ship Comes Sailing In

'I spy a ship approaching,' cried a lookout.

'Is it bristling?' shouted Nettles.

'Bristling with oars,' replied the awed lookout. 'All dipping in and out of the water at the same time.'

'It's the invaders' ship all right,' said Nettles, grimly. 'Bearing not only the invaders, but the traitors, Finn, Pansy and Sage. No doubt those turncoats have told them of my plan to fight on these beaches when they try to land. Well, I intend to spring a surprise they'll choke on when they arrive.'

'What surprise would that be, Nettles?' asked eager Poppy. 'Could you spring it before the invaders arrive?'

'Surprises tend to be sprung at any time,' said Nettles, wisely. 'I might order a pretend retreat and then fall on the enemy while they are confused. I'll call it my circling action.'

'That sounds like a piece of Berrybottom's advice,' worried Poppy. Then she brightened. 'But only a fool would follow his advice, and you're no fool, Nettles.'

But it was too late for Nettles to juggle his plans. Events were moving faster than his brain could think.

'The invaders are now shipping their oars and steering in,' cried the lookout. 'Any moment now their vessel will be grinding on to the sands of our beach. Is our future safe in the hands of our new leader Nettles, I wonder? Can he cope with this desperate crisis, we all tremble to ask? We can only hope that he proves to be worthy of our trust. This is your lookout signing off, as I scramble down to join the battle, filled with hope and dread.'

In fact, Nettles had decided that he would have to make do and mend, thinking up a new plan of defence as he went along. Quickly he ordered the warriors to form a strong semi-circle around the landing point with their weapons at the ready. Then, with Poppy, Umber and Amber, he strode to the centre to take up his position as their fighting general.

Unfortunately there was an obstacle in the way. Berrybottom had chosen to squat himself down on the beach where the fighting was bound to take place, and there he sat like a sore thumb, bathing his filthy toes in the ripples of the stream, blissfully unaware of the dangerous situation now unfolding. It was too late to order him to the rear, to join the cheering youngsters and the baggage. Nettles decided angrily to let the fool of The Briars stay there if he was determined to be killed. Meanwhile he and his grim-faced band stood their ground as the prow of the invader ship crunched into the sand, making them feel very small in the huge shadow it threw.

'Make every arrow and sword-thrust count, brave warriors,' shouted Nettles. 'Here on this beach we'll stand or fall! And if right is might we'll win this battle. But should we be defeated then let our histories record that we died with honour to save our beloved valley. I notch this arrow to my bow . . . a barb to bring the enemy low . . . but should I fall in pain and woe . . . still battle on, I order so . . .'

From the rear came the sound of clapping as Meadowsweet expressed her admiration for Nettles' poetic words. Even cynical Teasel looked impressed.

Now the defenders could clearly see the scarred and savage faces of the invaders as they peered down from the side of the ship. Also plain to see were the gleaming axes they brandished, whetted and sharpened to taste fresh blood. Yet their faces betrayed a nervousness that puzzled the defenders. Why hadn't they leapt overboard to attack at once? Why did they hesitate?

The answers came from a tiny bird and a trio of sad and bloodied traitors. But were they really traitors? Nettles was torn between sympathy and anger as they gazed imploringly down from the deck at him. Finn tried to speak, but the suffering he had endured made his words a whispered croak. Pansy and Sage were also trying to plead their innocence from their floating prison. But their words were snatched away by the sounds of bellowed orders, the stowing away of heavy oars and the rasp of steel axes being sharpened. Then Jenny flew down from the deck to perch on Berrybottom's tousled head. She spoke, furiously winking one eye at the bewildered Nettles. She looked very cocky and pleased with herself.

'Dear companion for life, I'm pleased to

announce that the plundering and the slaying has been put on hold for a while,' she chirped. 'The much feared Captain Olaf Ruff has agreed to spare the valley while he meets with the powerful wizard Berrybottom, the very person who happens to be squatting under my claws. Ruff is staying his hand because he is sore afraid of something he doesn't understand.'

'I'm sore suspicious, you mean,' bellowed a voice. Then the menacing figure of Ruff appeared on the prow of the ship. His long red hair streamed in the wind as he gazed down to sneer at the scruffy figure sitting on the sand. 'So that is Berrybottom, who has the power to make us shake in our sea-boots! Well, let's see what *he* can do, before I show him what *I* can do. Let's see the colour of his so-called magic. But be warned, if his boast is a bluff, you lot on that beach will pay dearly for it. I'm just a twitch of my finger away from hurling my crew into action. They've long known about, and lusted for the golden snake who glitters on the hill. They won't be cheated of that prize by a trick. For their thirst for gold can't be controlled, when once I let them loose. So, let the mighty Berrybottom demonstrate his powers. Let him make a test-case of my cabin-boy if he's a genuine wizard.'

'You're doing it again, Ollie,' wept Ossie. 'Why am I always the scape-toad? Why am I always chosen to be the sample and the example? I'm only on board to make beds and sweep decks. Now I'm about to be turned into a toad, to hop around for ever on a lonely foreign shore!'

'Be quiet,' snarled Ruff. 'This is warrior business.'

'Then step ashore and make it so,' challenged Nettles. 'We're ready to do the business whenever you are, brutal Ruff. And what Berrybottom has to do with this fight, I've no idea.'

'Berrybottom could be the chink in their armour, Nettles,' Finn shouted down. 'He might have the power to save our valley. At least you should give him the chance to try.'

'And here the mighty one is, in all his glory,'

giggled Jenny, pointing her beak downwards. 'Itching and scratching, ready to weave his potent spells, a silly blank grin on his face.'

'Absolute nonsense,' cried Poppy, standing at Nettles' side, her dagger drawn. 'Take no notice, my leader! Our enemies are just trying to confuse us. Especially the three traitors aboard that ship.'

'Yet Ruff and his crew hesitate,' said Nettles, puzzled. 'I think another plan is beginning to form in my mind. If Captain Ruff and his invaders are really afraid of Berrybottom . . .'

'You think *I'm* afraid of *him*?' shouted Ruff, roaring with laughter. 'Afraid of that poor idiot sitting in the sand, and playing with his toes? Why, I'm more afraid of my cabin-boy!'

'Not as afraid as I am of you, Ollie,' said Ossie, quickly. 'I've been desperately afraid of you from the moment I stepped aboard this ship.'

'Don't be fooled by the innocent appearance of Berrybottom,' warned Jenny. 'He can be deadly if provoked.'

'Let's just test how deadly,' challenged Ruff,

hefting his sharp war axe. His nervous crew gave a mighty cheer, relieved that their chief was in charge again.

'What are we waiting for?' cried Umber, fretting at Nettles' side. 'The talking and the taunting is over. Let us attack and storm the ship. One thing is certain, those vandals will never touch a single scale of our Great Golden Snake!'

'And not one maiden will they carry off back to the northlands,' vowed Poppy and Amber, 'for they must have lots of nice girls at home.'

'We advise you to row back to where you came from,' yelled the warriors on the shore. 'Because you won't set one foot upon this beach!'

'And who's going to stop us?' sneered Ruff. 'Certainly not you pathetic lot. As for the idiot squatting in the sand, he scares us not at all. Where are his powerful spells, for we've yet to see one.'

Then with contempt on his face he snatched up a spare axe and hurled it. Sharp and glittering, it spun through the air missing Berrybottom by a whisker.

That was Ruff's big mistake. He had dared to spoil Berrybottom's new-found happiness. And the wizard of The Briars knew how to deal with folk who made him miserable, as his ex-wives knew.

Scrambling to his feet, he pulled from his scratchy tunic the flint he used for making fire. Then he gathered some dry bits of driftwood and soon had a crackling blaze going. Filling his spell-pot from the stream he brought it to a merry boil, and delving into his ingredients pouch, he began to toss disgusting objects into the brew.

Was he preparing his toad-spell, or his vanishing one? Could he actually do something right this time? Could he be the first of many generations of Berrybottoms to get a spell perfectly right? A spell that succeeded completely, instead of only partly? Judging by the determination on his craggy face, Ruff and his crew were going to suffer for interfering with the happiness he had only recently found.

Meanwhile, his every action had been watched

in wide-eyed silence by those on the ship and those on the shore. Were they seeing a genuine wizard in action, or just a fraud going through some mesmerizing motions?

One small person was in no doubt. Ossie the cabin-boy had been watching with mounting terror, as Berrybottom scurried about his magical business. Suddenly, yelling with fear, he leapt over the side of the ship to land with a splash in the water. Then as quick as a crab he darted to huddle close to Berrybottom, his eyes filled with pleading.

'Please, let me be your friend, oh mighty Berrybottom,' he begged. 'Let me be your humble assistant for the rest of my life. I'm too young and innocent to be turned into a toad or vanished from the face of the earth when I've only just started to live!'

For a moment Berrybottom looked puzzled. He had never experienced such instant devotion. But having been short of devotees all his life, he welcomed it. Giving Ossie a hug and a craggy grin, he returned to the task in hand. The horrible mixture in his pot was bubbling furiously as he stood over it and began to make fluttering movements with his horny hands – like proper wizards did! As he went through these motions the invaders began to fidget nervously, for they feared the deeds of darkness. Their grandmothers had schooled them well to beware the black arts.

Meanwhile, on the shore Nettles and his warriors watched with growing hope and expectation. Perhaps the scorned Berrybottom could rid them of their enemies after all!

The tension mounted as the wizard of The Briars began to chant. It was an angry chant to remind everyone that Berrybottom hated to be made unhappy when he had found happiness at last. His angry voice was joined by the piping tones of Ossie, who was clinging to the wizard's itchy tunic for comfort. For the little cabin-boy had burned his boat behind him and would stick to his new master Berrybottom, come what may. The call of the sea had long palled for him, and he disliked Captain Olaf Ruff more than words could say. Now, at last, he could shout insults and threats at Ollie while his new master Berrybottom spelled them out . . .

'May the foes of Berrybottom,
May all Berrybottom's foes,
Vanish in a flash of magic
From their tips down to their toes . . .'

The result came with a puff of orange and green smoke from the pot. For a few brief moments the battleground was stilled except for the wildly thudding hearts on both sides of the stubborn divide. Then Ruff and his crew appeared to shimmer, before turning into a whiter shade of pale. Nettles and his warriors gaped in wonder at this demonstration of Berrybottom's wizardly power. Unfortunately, moments later Ruff and his crew appeared in sharp and menacing colour again. In anger or through haste Berrybottom had botched his vanishing spell again. And in full view of critical witnesses too! There was not even a toad in sight to prove he had spelled anything half-right. He had managed to send his ex-wives into the land of neither here nor there, so why not these enemies also? What could have gone wrong? But he had no time to ponder as the invaders began to recover from their attacks of giddiness. Soon they were jeering and shouting war-cries as they stormed over the side of the ship to do battle with the defenders of the beach.

'Let not one enemy remain alive,' roared Ruff, planting his sturdy legs on the sand and whirling his war axe around his head. 'Especially that phoney wizard and Oswald, my treacherous cabin-boy!'

His frightening words were enough for Berrybottom. Snatching up his possessions he dashed from the sands and into the trees. Ruff's fury was also enough for Ossie the turncoat cabin-boy. Howling in terror, he hared after Berrybottom, his new master, determined to stick to him like glue. Soon they had vanished into the thick green trees and out of harm's way. Bound together as fugitives, thus they would stay, perhaps to return, to spell another day. As they plunged deeper into the undergrowth the evil laughter of Berrybottom's ghostly wives echoed in their ears . . .

'You can run, but you cannot hide from us, wicked husband,' they cackled. 'Soon we'll track down the vital ingredient needed to perfect the spell that no Berrybottom has ever mastered. Then with the greatest of pleasure we'll vanish you from the face of the earth for ever . . . Oh, how sweet will revenge taste,' they screeched after the scrambling, sweating pair. 'And we'll be there to watch you fade away, a joy beyond compare . . .'

Thirteen

THE BATTLE OF BUTTERCUP HILL

There was no time for clever plans now. Nettles
and his warriors stood shoulder to shoulder
as they prepared for a bitter fight. Swords were
drawn and arrows notched to bows. A tense
silence fell over the opposing forces, broken only
by the trilling of a lark rising high into the sky
that beautiful spring morning. Though ordered

to do so, Poppy and Amber had refused to go to the rear to join the youngsters and the baggage. Daggers drawn they stood in the front rank beside Nettles and Umber, prepared to retreat not one step. Their faces told it all. The female of the People was as deadly as the male when danger threatened. The grim expression on Poppy's face belied her primrosed hat, the flowers now beginning to wilt. Skilled at slicing vegetables, she was just as ready to slice an enemy who threatened the beloved valley of the People. Amber was equally determined. She was prepared to give her life to defend the Great Golden Snake who lay sleeping on the hill.

The invaders stood shoulder to shoulder, hefting their sharp axes and glowering back at the People who stood in their way to the fabulous wealth of the snake that coiled around this rich valley. Then there was a small scuffle from behind them as Finn and Pansy and Sage took advantage of the lull before the battle to escape, to rush to join their Willow family.

'Now we'll prove that we aren't traitors,' cried Finn. 'Give us weapons so that we can fight at your side, Nettles!'

'Poppy, have you got a spare dagger under your cloak?' pleaded Pansy. 'Even if it's only your old vegetable knife. Give it to me, for this is no time to argue about our stations in life.'

'And here am I, my Nettles,' gasped Sage, pushing her furry body into the front rank of the warriors. 'Ever faithful unto death. As faithful as my father before me. Call me misguided, my friend, but never a traitor!'

'I've misjudged you all,' cried Nettles, bitterly. 'Please forgive me. If I should die then mourn me as a brother who judged in haste!'

'This is all very noble, Nettles,' snapped Jenny from her perch on a nearby rock. 'But words don't win battles. So let's get on with it before you all die from hoarse throats!'

What terrible, mocking words were those. To prove why he was so feared, Ruff took a pace forward and hurled his war axe with deadly aim at a warrior standing in the front row of the defenders. The brave soldier fell to the sand, his head split in two and spurting blood. Then Ruff drew his keen stabbing sword and charged, bellowing for his men to follow, to be pitiless in their spilling of blood.

'You desire gold, then fight for it!' he yelled. 'You yearn to be acclaimed as heroes when we return home, then kill for that honour! And should one of you hang back from this battle, then even in my bloody tatters I'll seek you out and slit your throat. So follow me, my lusty rascals! And shame on he who first turns tail!'

Their yelling charge was met by a shower of arrows from the defenders. A few barbs found their mark, but there was no stopping the maddened invaders. They were determined to draw close, to bring their deadly axes into play. The clash, when it came, was grim and shocking. Despite their brave efforts, the swords and the arrows of Nettles and his band had little effect against the murderous war axes swinging in unison, as the enemy pressed home their attack. Then Finn fell, blood streaming from a savage wound. As Pansy desperately tried to shield him, she too was slashed by a glancing axe-stroke. They lay together, unstirring. Realizing the futility of such close combat Nettles made a wise decision for so young a leader. It was also a compassionate one, as he saw his comrades falling around him. His voice rang out above the shouts and the clash of weapons.

'Fall back, my warriors, but keep good order,' he cried. 'Archers, advance and fire off your arrows to cover the retreat. This is not a defeat but a backward ploy to strengthen our position! We'll fight the decisive battle on the slopes of Buttercup Hill!'

As they began to fall back, Ruff and his crew scented victory. They surged forward, only to be cowed by another flight of stinging arrows. By now the defenders were fighting in small groups, pressing back the enemy, while their comrades dashed to reform in the rear. It was a deadly game of leapfrog that Nettles and his warriors were playing as they were driven from the beach. Soon they were battling on the green turf that grew beneath the home oak.

The terrible sounds of battle struck fear into the hearts of the Willow Clan going about their business high in the tree. They quickly hurried from their network of homes and halls carved inside the mighty boughs of the oak. Hiding behind curtains of leaves they gazed in horror at the vicious fight taking place below. They had placed their confidence in Nettles, their new leader, who would surely solve the problem of the barbarian ship. So what had gone wrong? Their terror increased to see that Nettles and his warriors were being driven back towards Buttercup Hill by a howling horde of northerners wielding their blood-stained axes about them.

Then came an incident that made the gentle Willow folk shake with dread. A tall red-haired savage – he could only be the leader – looked up at the branches of the tree and shook his gory axe, a wicked leer on his scarred face. The gesture was plain. It said that when Nettles and his warriors had been destroyed, then the folk in the oak would be the next victims to taste the fury of his wrath. Then the confused battle moved on. But not before a distressed and angry Granny Willow had shouted down to have her say. Her words were addressed to Nettles, who was desperately fighting his rearguard action, his face smeared with blood and sweat and also some tears for the fallen friends left behind.

'Oh, foolish boy,' she wailed. 'You were so safe amongst my pots and pans. Is this what your ambition has led you to? An early death against a long life in my kitchen? Yet I know that you fight to save our valley from evil. So may you still triumph and come safe home, each and every one. My stew will always be simmering, piping hot, glorious return or not.'

But her words went unheeded as the opposing forces vanished from view, heading for a reckoning on Buttercup Hill. The old lady had to restrain Rosie and Thorn by grabbing the scruffs of their necks, or they would have climbed down the tree to follow after their heroes.

Meanwhile, back on the beach peace reigned again. The dead lay weeping blood into the stream. Strangely, amongst that sadness there was no sign of Finn and Pansy. The bodies of the fisherboy and his loyal Pansy were puzzlingly absent. As for the trilling lark, its joyous flight to reach Heaven was long over. Now it sat contented on its nest, clucking as sweet as any song. While high above, the sun shone bright and reached its peak midday, so up a hill a figure raced to spread more deep dismay . . .

It was Sage who scurried to break the news to the Guardians on the hill. Ordered by Nettles, she had broken away from the battle to warn them of the danger that threatened. By this time the uproar of conflict could clearly be heard on the hill, and it was coming closer. At once many willing hands were reaching for weapons, even sticks and stones, for anything was better than nothing when it came to the defence of their great snake and their hilltop home. The volunteers rushed to peer downwards. They saw the afternoon sun glinting on the grappling swords and axes, saw their hard-pressed friends being driven ever upwards by the overwhelming power of their enemies. Seeing the danger of the situation they needed no command, no rallying cry. As one the Guardians charged down the hill to enter the fray.

Though they fought valiantly, their help was not enough to sway the bitter contest. For when blood was their argument, the northern invaders were experts at spilling it. A lust for blood and gold, that was their driving force. Ruff seemed to be everywhere on the battlefield, threatening and cajoling his men to greater effort. The end of the unequal fight had to come, and so it did.

Nettles and his warriors finally broke on the brow of Buttercup Hill. Defeated but still defiant, they retreated to the head of the Great Golden Snake and gathered about its huge, snoozing nose. Sheltering behind them were the gentle Guardian people, wondering what fate had in store for them, as they gazed at the brutish faces of Ruff's victorious men.

'Throw down your weapons,' roared Ruff, panting heavily. 'Or be butchered on the spot by my merciless crew! From this moment you are all our cringing slaves. For we won't be denied the gold that we've fought so hard and killed for. As from now, the task for you all will be to dismantle that golden snake and hurry the treasure back to our ship in sacks of nuggets!'

'We also demand a few pretty maidens,' reminded a crew member. He grinned. 'I notice that some of them are eyeing me already.'

'Oh no we're not!' cried the outraged Guardian girls. 'We're eyeing you with contempt and hatred. Anyway, you northern men are much too ugly for us!'

'You don't understand,' pleaded Umber, limping forward. 'Our great snake is not made of *real* gold. He's a living, breathing creature.'

'Don't try your tricks on me,' bellowed Ruff. 'I know true glittering gold when I see it. Lads, advance and hack off a few sample nuggets.'

The eager crew dashed forward, their axes swinging. As their fearsome weapons bit deep into the golden, scaly skin they received the shock of their lives. The eyes of the sleeping giant suddenly flicked open and he uttered a long sigh of pain. At the same time, a tremor rippled down his enormous body, coiled around the valley of the People like an eternal band of gold. Trickles of bright red blood began to ooze from the wounds inflicted by a dozen sharp axes. The crew drew back in horror and fear – tinged with bitter disappointment. For their dream of great wealth was seeping away before their eyes. Soon they were muttering and casting dark glances at Captain Ruff. Hadn't he promised them bountiful booty from this voyage?

Ruff felt suddenly afraid. His men were still in fighting mood and they were looking for a scapegoat, someone to blame. And it seemed that he was in line for that title if he didn't do something, and quickly. A mutiny at sea he could cope with. But a mutiny on land he had never had to deal with. He knew that his command – and even his life – were at stake if he failed to regain control. All at once he was the swaggering tyrant again, as he addressed the beaten foe, his bloody axe resting on his muscled shoulder.

'So, your fabled snake is mere flesh and blood after all,' he snarled at Umber. 'But we still demand gold. We don't care where it comes from, so long as there's enough to overflow the hold of our ship. For we won't leave this valley empty-handed. We'd sooner leave it a smoking wasteland, heaped with your dead bodies.'

'To return to the northlands with an empty hold would make us a laughing-stock,' cried an angry sailor, 'making our grandmothers ashamed of us!'

'And we'd look foolish in the eyes of the pretty maidens we hope to marry,' yelled another. 'They'd scorn us as failures. They'd say, "What's the use of a swashbuckling sea dog, if he isn't rich with gold?" '

'Nasty sea dogs, you mean,' shouted Meadowsweet. 'You wicked invaders will go down in my history notes as the ogres you are! I'm thinking of writing a damning poem about you all. Then your grandmothers will truly wash their hands of you!'

'This isn't the time for a history lesson,' hissed Teasel, nudging her. 'This is the real world and not our quiet library!'

'Give us the signal, and we'll fall upon the invaders, Umber,' cried the young Guardians. 'Our bodies are honed to fitness, thanks to all the dragging of heavy stones to build our Snakehenge. Our horny hands will soon throttle the life from their throats!'

'Go back to the fireside and your mothers,' said Amber, sternly. 'This is a grown-up problem, best faced by we grown-ups.'

Then Nettles stepped forward to confront the glowering Ruff. Ever a shadow at his side was

Poppy, her hat dented and askew, but defiantly still in place. Though wincing in pain from his wounds, the boy spoke firmly.

'You have defeated us in battle, Captain Ruff,' he said. 'We bow to your superior force. As for the large amounts of gold that you demand, we People of the valley can only offer what we have. I promise that every soul from every home will pool every scrap of treasure they have to help fill the hold of your ship. It won't be much but it's the best we can do. But if you refuse my offer I have another solution. You and I will fight in single combat, to the death. And whoever wins will show compassion for his former foes.'

'We didn't sail here for trinkets, stupid boy,' scoffed Ruff. 'Your offer is brushed aside as I'd brush *you* aside, should we fight. My crew and I will settle for no less than a staggering amount of gold that could sink our ship if not properly stowed in the hold.'

'That amount of gold doesn't exist in the whole of our valley,' protested Poppy. 'We live simple lives, save for the flamboyance of a fashionable hat here and there.'

'And we Guardians love our great snake for his golden heart,' cried Amber. 'Not for the colour of his earthly body!'

'Our dreams are turning sour, Captain Ruff,' muttered the crew. 'We've endured your savage kicks and lashings. But only because you promised us vast riches. Be warned, should your promise backfire, *we'll* be doing the kicking and lashing on the voyage back home, and guess who'll be on the receiving end?'

'Excuse me,' chirped a cheery voice. 'If I may interrupt your friendly heart to heart discussion? But I think I can help you all.'

It was Jenny. She had flown in from somewhere or other to perch upon a twig. Being the deceitful kind of bird she was, her mission had probably been some secret spying and gathering of information. She was her usual mischievous self as she looked down on the tense scene through twinkling black eyes. She continued, addressing

Ruff who was looking increasingly afraid.

'If it's gold you're after, Berrybottom is the name,' she teased. 'He has great hoards of it misered away by generations of Berrybottoms past. They might have been a long line of failed wizards, but they did extremely well as far as riches were concerned. Sadly it was with wives that they had no luck, bless their poor nagged souls.'

'Didn't I promise you gold, lads?' cried delighted Ruff. 'Our dreams are about to come true. Now, will you forgive me for the savage kicks and lashings I dealt out during our arduous voyage? Just remember, it was my sternness as your captain that sailed us here to the brink of untold riches!'

'Forgiveness doesn't come so easy,' said a cautious crewman. 'The question is, what if Berrybottom's gold proves to be a myth like the gold of that great, idle snake?'

'The wizard's gold is no myth, I assure you,' grinned Jenny. 'Being the nosy type, I know exactly where the treasure of the Berrybottoms is hidden.'

'Then tell us where it is!' menaced Ruff. 'Tell us where that idiot wizard hides his family gold!'

'That's for you to find out,' chirped Jenny. 'I'm keeping my secret for the time being. Making things easy for folk is not in my nature. But I'm prepared to set you on the right track. For instance, I could tell you exactly where Berrybottom and Ossie, his new apprentice wizard, are hiding out. My suggestion is, that with a little persuasion, he would tell you where the gold is hidden.'

'With my hands around his throat he would!' roared Ruff. 'And I'd also make short work of that treacherous cabin-boy of mine. So where are the pair to be found, spying bird?'

'Not so fast,' said Jenny, coolly. 'First of all, you must meet a certain demand, otherwise there's no deal. You and your men must promise not to slaughter the folk of this valley, down to the last, innocent, fried baby.'

'And you must promise to leave us maidens alone,' cried the Guardian girls. 'We don't want to sail north with the ugly likes of you!'

'Agreed,' said Ruff, impatiently. 'So where are those two wretches hiding out? And no lies, cunning bird.'

'I've lied already,' giggled Jenny. 'When I said that I knew where the two were hiding out. I should have said four, all huddled together for comfort. But I'm saying no more for the time being.'

'How can you betray the hiding place of desperate fugitives?' said Nettles, scathingly. 'Even though it *will* save the lives of the rest of us. The shame of it! Who'd want to be a leader at such a time?'

'You did,' mocked Jenny. 'And you are that leader, thanks to me. So don't get all noble on me, companion of my life. One fights with the mind when the sword proves useless. Anyway, you never liked Berrybottom, so why the concern?'

'Spare us the soul-baring stuff,' snapped Ruff.

'Just tell us what we want to know. And remember, change your minds, and my men and I will be changing our direction of attack. There's a certain oak tree down in the valley that's ripe for pillaging. And we'll storm it with fire and bloody axe if you refuse to tell us the whereabouts of the two miserable creatures we seek.'

'In fact, four miserable creatures by my reckoning,' giggled Jenny. 'But that surprise can wait awhile. So what's our answer, Nettles my leader?'

Nettles needed only to look around to make his decision. His heart went out to the wounded and bloodied warriors who had fought so hard for him and their families. Though they thronged loyally around him, it was plain to see that they were totally spent. Amongst their ragged numbers he saw the terrified faces of Poppy, Umber, and Amber, those brave friends who still stood stubbornly by his side. But their fear was obvious, as indeed his own must be. Nettles knew what he had to do.

'To save the many, we have to sacrifice the two,' he said, sadly. 'Tell Ruff what he wants to know, Jenny wren. Then fly from my sight for ever. For my trust in you as a friend has gone.'

'There's grateful,' bristled the bird. 'You'd still be washing dishes if it wasn't for me! But I'll forgive your cruel words because of my love for you. And so, back to business. Are you ordering me to lead Captain Ruff and his mad axe-men to the hiding place of Berrybottom the fraud wizard, and Ossie the traitor who deserted his ship – which is also the refuge of the two other fugitives I've hinted at?'

'Yes, please just go,' answered weary Nettles. 'And may the histories of the People view me in a better light than the dark one in which I stand.'

'You'll always be *my* guiding light, dear Nettles,' said Jenny, her black eyes glowing. Then perkily she hopped around on her twig and spoke to glowering Ruff and his impatient men. Her voice was shrill, and her eyes twinkled with glee. 'So, are you ready for the gold rush, my lusty lads?

Fall down and worship me if you wish! For I am the key to the hoard of treasure you crave. Gold enough to fill the holds of six of your raiding ships! But tell me, is bowing out of fashion in the place where you've sailed from?'

The hint was quickly taken. Ruff and his men bowed humbly before the strutting little bird. If looks could kill she would have toppled dead from her twig. But Jenny only grinned. She loved the thrill of danger when she held the upper hand.

'So let's away to a secret place I know,' she cried. 'Where Berrybottom trembles, where Ossie the deserter quakes, where two mourned souls lie fighting death in order to cling on to life! Quite a sad scene, don't you think?'

'Just shut your beak and lead us there,' snapped Ruff. 'Unless you want us to butcher everyone on this hill and in that oak tree below. We northern raiders need little excuse to start swinging our axes again. Would you wish the death of so many on your conscience, vexing bird?'

'It's not a wish I relish,' said Jenny, glancing

around at the anxious faces of Nettles, his defeated warriors and the Guardian folk, still clutching their little ones tightly to them. 'Especially the picture of innocent babies being fried in your pans. Your wish is my command, Captain Olaf Ruff.'

'I also have a wish,' cried Meadowsweet, pointing her writing quill at Ruff. 'And that is for Berrybottom finally to get his spells right, and turn you all into hopping toads! Or, better still, vanish you completely with a masterpiece of magic!'

'Hold your tongue,' hissed Teasel, nudging her. 'Just let your scribbling do the talking. You're just the kind of pretty maiden they'll kidnap and take back north if you make yourself known and noticed!'

'And you'd be the last one to try to save me!' retorted the girl. But she wisely returned to her parchment, determined to write down every word and every action she had witnessed throughout that terrible day. For if she lived she meant to write her *Great History of the Valley of the People* for future generations to ponder and to gasp at the genius of her words – and gape at her beauty too, for she intended to grace the cover of her work with a portrait of herself. As she wrote, so she glanced between squiggles at scowling Ruff, her expression one of cool contempt.

Shamed by her defiance Nettles limped forward to confront the raider captain. He felt very small as he looked up at his muscular enemy. He was also awed. Could eyes be so blue, yet so cold and unfeeling? Could a mane of wild hair be so red without bursting into flame? But from so close, one thing was perfectly plain. In spite of his savage appearance, Ruff's nose was tellingly upturned. Which meant that he was of the People, however alien and remote. Yet there was not a flicker of recognition in Ruff's icy eyes as he stared down at the boy. It seemed that time and space had severed any bond that might have been between them. Then Nettles found his courage and spoke for everyone in the valley as a true leader should.

'When your hold is filled with gold, then will you sail away?' he demanded to know. 'You've won the battle of Buttercup Hill, but I vow you'll lose the next clash if you force it. We valley folk will rally twice as fiercely, if you push us to the brink. To defend our way of life we'll fight you tooth and nail, even down to our last dying breath.'

'You're in no position to threaten us,' snarled Ruff.

'And there's something else,' said Nettles, growing bolder. 'If Berrybottom has a hidden hoard of gold, then take it. But we demand that you spare his life. You must also spare the life of Ossie, who fled with him into the woods. For his only offence was to desert your ship when your cruelty became too much to bear.'

'Don't forget the other two fugitives clinging to life,' interrupted Jenny. 'They also cower in the secret place only I know about. I won't lead you to Berrybottom unless all four are spared.'

Ruff was prepared to agree to anything just to

get his hands on Berrybottom's gold. But his cunning mind was already making future plans. Once the hold of his ship was filled, he would show this pathetic rabble just how vengeful he could be. He would leave this valley a ravaged desert before he sailed for home. Then, once there, he would be acclaimed as a great hero, hopefully by his grandma who had nursed him in the contented days of his childhood.

'On my honour, I promise to spare the lives of all four fugitives in return for the gold,' he said, solemnly. 'And I hope that everyone will forgive me for being quick tempered sometimes. But it's my faithful crew I'm always thinking about. Having been poor for so long, I'm anxious to make them rich for the first time in their lives.'

This was balm to the crew, who had always believed that Ruff thought only of himself. Delighted, they began to dance a jig upon the hill.

'The bare-faced nerve of that ruffian Ruff!' gasped Meadowsweet, scribbling down his weasel words. 'He's done nothing but lie since he rowed here! And we have to trust in those lies, because we have no choice if we hope to save our valley. I intend to end my great work with a moral, Teasel. Better to earn gold from the sweat of your brow than steal it from the brows of others!'

'That'll make your future readers think deeply,' grinned her fellow librarian. 'And close your great book with a dusty bang!'

'So, Captain Ruff,' said Poppy, looking him squarely in the eye. 'You've put your honour on the line to keep your every word. If you go back on it, you'll never be able to look yourself in the face again. Do you realize that?'

'Yes, yes,' snapped Ruff. 'The gold is all we want. Once we have it, we'll sail away for ever.'

'Does that apply to you all?' said Nettles, looking at the smiling, jigging crew. 'The gold and nothing more?'

'We swear on the lives of our grandmothers,' vowed the rascally crew. 'And what is more sacred than that?'

'Nothing,' agreed Nettles. 'I would never take

the name of my Granny Willow in vain. So, Jenny wren, guide Ruff and his men to the place where the fugitives cower. Reassure them that their lives are not in danger. And tell Berrybottom that the life of everyone in our valley depends on him surrendering to Ruff his family hoard of hidden treasure. Don't let me down, Jenny, for your behaviour of late has been more than a little suspect, as if you're playing some sort of double game. Just obey my orders this time. Unless you wish to sink lower in my esteem.'

'Pardon my little lapses, beloved leader,' apologized Jenny. 'But I've had to deal with crisis after crisis just lately! I promise to be the model of faithfulness from this time on.'

'So, are we going Berrybottom-hunting or not?' bellowed Ruff. 'Be warned, I'm having to hold my men in check. They're beginning to practise their axe-swings again!'

'Lead away, Jenny,' ordered Nettles, then to Ruff, 'Just remember the promises you've made, that no harm will come to anyone when you discover the secret hiding place. Even a villain like you wouldn't go back on his solemn word of honour.'

'Just heap your hold with gold and go away,' cried Poppy. 'And when you put to sea I hope you sink under the weight of your stolen booty!'

'Just go, and good riddance,' yelled Umber and Amber. 'Never to darken the dreams of our great snake again!'

'And a warm goodbye to you, too,' smiled Ruff with a rare flash of humour. Then he turned to ridicule Nettles. 'I hear that *you* once scrubbed dishes in a kitchen. There must be a huge pile waiting for you now. Perhaps if you hurry you might get your old job back, for leader you certainly are not!'

Before angry Nettles could retort, Ruff had turned his broad back and was marshalling his men into line. Then, with Jenny fluttering overhead, the raiders shouldered their axes and marched down Buttercup Hill, unmoved by the bloody carnage that littered their way. As they marched, they roared a chant, in time with the tramp of their sea boots . . .

> 'What do we want?
> Heaps of gold,
> When do we want it?
> Now . . .'

'Now we can only hope and pray,' said grim-faced Nettles, 'that Berrybottom agrees to give up his treasure for the sake of our sacred valley.'

'Such a small price to pay for peace,' murmured hopeful Poppy.

'Yet how high the price already?' wept gentle Sage. 'With so many wounded and dead on both sides.'

The afternoon grew chilly as the sun sank in the sky. The Guardians began to stoke up their fires and comfort their frightened and bewildered small ones. Then, as always, they tended to the needs of their Great Golden Snake. Silverfish and honey were placed under his nose, should he stir from his sleep feeling peckish. But he was snoring as sweetly as ever, perhaps dreaming of a time when the valley was young, a time before the People came, when the stars were the only companions of his loneliness.

'We must go home now, Umber,' said Nettles. 'We're worried about our family. Like yours they'll be terribly distressed by the events of today. But we're only down the hill should you need us.'

'And we're only up the hill should *your* need be greater,' said Umber, attempting a wry grin. 'Let's hope that our worries will be sailing away when a new dawn breaks . . .'

As the wearied and battle-scarred Willow folk trudged off down the hill, Nettles whispered a few words into Sage's ear. With a nod of her whiskered nose she slipped quietly away. Wending their way down Buttercup Hill to their home oak tree, the party shed many unashamed tears at the piteous sights they saw along the way . . .

Fourteen

No Hiding Place

After their terrified flight from the beach and into the woods, Berrybottom and Ossie blundered straight into a large tangle of brambles. For the wizard of The Briars it was almost home from home, his leathery skin being well used to cuts and scratches. But for a small cabin-boy it was pure torture, as the sharp thorns ripped through his thin tunic and into his flesh. For a long while they lay hidden, panting to recover their breath, their ears alert for the sounds of pursuit. Save for the twitter of a disturbed bird and the odd cough or growl of a prowling animal, there seemed no cause for alarm. The relief they felt soon calmed their thumping hearts. Eventually they fell asleep.

Some time later they were roused with a start by the sound of voices and stumbling around the entrance to their hideout. Then came the sound of thrashing foliage and the fugitives began to tremble again. Were they about to be discovered? Was the dreaded enemy without, trying to get in? Both of them were in no doubt that Ruff would kill them without mercy, should he get his bloody hands on them. They could only cling together and await their fate as a shaft of light lit up the small crawl-space that led to the centre of the bramble patch. Then came the sound of voices again.

'This will be our refuge,' someone whispered.

'We'll squeeze inside and rest awhile. A few more scratches won't hurt us, after all we've been through. Then when we've tended our wounds, we'll think of what to do. Come, lean on me, we'll soon be safe and sound in this thick, dark hiding place.'

The fugitives inside their den instantly relaxed, for the voice was that of a girl, and one known to them. Eagerly they crawled to meet the incomers. Soon they were helping them into the shelter of their snug haven. It soon became clear that while Pansy was suffering from a blow to her head, Finn was the more badly injured. His leg was broken and crudely splinted with his own sword. He also had deep slashes to his arms and shoulders in urgent need of attention.

It was then that Berrybottom came into his own. The gold hoarder, the phoney wizard of magic spells and potions went swiftly to work. Reaching into his ingredients pouch he took out some smelly ointments and bundles of dried herbs. The ointments he gently smeared over Finn and

Pansy's open wounds. Just like a real wizard he waved his gnarled hands in the air, while muttering some mystic words. Then he carefully re-set Finn's broken leg, dressing it with herbs and a stout bramble stem for a splint. Then followed more fluttering of hands and mumbo-jumbo. The final part of his cure was to give each of them a pinch of magic mushroom powder which they swallowed dutifully. Almost immediately, Finn and Pansy began to feel much better. Happy even. But the four were well aware that they were not yet out of trouble. The first trouble arrived with the sound of even more voices, but these voices were not distressed ones – in fact, they were gleeful and filled with hatred. Words and hideous cackling seemed to be drifting from a nearby bush, as was the choking smoke from a small fire . . .

'Hide where you will, but we'll always find you, Berrybottom,' taunted Nightshade, the first of his cast-off wives. 'Even from this ghostly world into which you spelled us, we can still track you down and haunt you. Can you smell the pungency of our bubbling pot, you cringing hollow worm? We're on the brink of finding the last ingredient that will vanish you for ever. We believe that it could be the root of a tiny rare flower that grows in shyness somewhere. And we'll find it, Berrybottom. And when we do, we'll add it to our brew and send you to dwell in the fires of Hell, till time ticks its last tock!'

'But first you'll be stripped of your earthly gold, you old miser,' cackled Leafmould, 'for we've spied a column of men with sharp axes marching towards these woods, and their boisterous chant is all about the hidden gold of Berrybottom, and what they intend to do if you won't give it up. It's not a pretty picture!'

'So despair, cruel husband,' screamed Sourseed, 'as we've despaired since you spelled us into this halfway land of limbo. For we know how you cherish gold above all things, including throwaway wives!'

'What gold?' cried terrified Berrybottom.

'I'm a very poor wizard, I am!'

'We know better, Berrybottom,' giggled Nightshade. 'We know why the pool at The Briars shines so brightly golden. The pool you never allowed *us* to bathe in.'

'We know why it glints when the sun rises and sets,' mocked Leafmould. 'And nothing is as certain as the searching sun.'

'Nor as certain as the moon,' hissed Sourseed, 'that every night reflects itself in the richness of your pond. The secret of you and your hoarding forebears was never a secret to we wives. But we kept that secret because . . . because . . .'

'Because we thought you married us for love,' cried Nightshade, sobbing for them all. 'And we'll never forgive you for casting us aside, you heartless wretch!'

Then they joined voices to sing a mournful song. The words expressed their deep hurt, but also the anger and the hatred they had stored for so long . . .

'You ruined the lives
Of three faithful wives,
Spelled out in the cold
For fresh faces and gold,
But remember us well
As you plummet to Hell
With no one to mourn you,
Farewell.'

'But that farewell will come later,' gloated the wives. 'In the meantime we still have much joy to look forward to. We're now going to hurry away to the scene of your crimes, Berrybottom, to await your coming there. For a villain always returns to the place where his shameful career began . . .'

And their voices and hysterical laughter drifted away as did the noxious smell from their simmering brew pot. For a while there was an awkward silence in the little den at the centre of the bramble patch. Then fear and curiosity won out.

'Who were those angry ladies you were talking

to?' asked Berrybottom's anxious companions. 'We could only see their flitting paleness through the roots of the brambles. And what did they mean about a column of axe men marching this way to demand your hidden gold? It can only mean that our hiding place has been betrayed!'

'Nothing to worry about,' said Berrybottom, forcing a smile. 'Those ghostly ladies were just a few nagging hags from my past, full of bitterness as all yesterday's wives are. As for the gold they spoke about, what gold I'd like to know? So why should a column of axe men march down on a simple wizard who's lived in poverty all his life? There's nothing to be concerned about, my friends. You've heard of old wives' tales, and this is just another one!'

But it was obvious to Finn, Pansy and shivering Ossie that the bitter argument with the ghostly ladies had shaken Berrybottom. He began to scratch himself as if the whole of his body was on fire. Uneasy glances were exchanged amongst the other three. Weakened from their wounds Finn and Pansy could only hope that the ghostly wives had been lying, and that their hideout would remain undiscovered until they were able to defend themselves again.

As for Ossie, in his twitchiness he was crawling around the close confines of the den. To calm his nerves he began to pluck at the small shoots pushing up through the earthen floor and count them soothingly. Then his eyes lit upon a beautiful sight glowing amongst the greenery of the brambles. It was a tiny red flower growing shyly in the shadows. Ossie gently stroked its crimson petals. In some mystical way, the action seemed to soothe his fears. On an impulse he grasped to pick the flower. His clumsiness pulled the whole plant from the earth, roots and all. He stared in wonder. If the tiny red bloom was beautiful, the root was even more so. It glowed luminous blue and pulsated as if charged by some inner force. The entranced cabin-boy stared at it for a long time. Then suddenly his friends were nudging him, to warn that someone was entering their hideout. With a quick unthinking motion Ossie stuffed the wonderful plant inside his tunic, and then he scrambled to join his fellow fugitives who were staring at the swishing passageway in trepidation. To their huge relief it was Sage, the gentle water-vole, whom everyone could trust. With her keen sense of smell she had sniffed them out. But she clearly had no time for welcomes. Her tone was urgent as she told them to listen closely.

'I've been sent here by our leader, Nettles,' she whispered, 'to bear his plea to Berrybottom. To save lives and to prevent the destruction of our valley, he implores the wizard of The Briars to deliver up his hoard of gold to the invaders who are marching this way. Their guide is the spy Jenny who watched you all scramble into this bramble patch. So, Berrybottom, will you sacrifice your gold in return for the peace we folk of the valley crave?'

'Why does everyone think I've got lots of gold?' blustered Berrybottom. 'I've never owned a single nugget in my life! My forebears and I have always offered potions and spells to those in need, almost free of charge. Why do folk keep spreading this lie that I'm a rich wizard?'

'Come clean about your wealth, Berrybottom, for there's not much time,' urged Sage. She cocked a sensitive ear. 'Even now I can hear the sound of tramping feet nearing this bush. Be warned, Ruff and his gold-rushing men won't question you so gently when they arrive.'

'The game's up, Berrybottom,' chirped a cheerful voice. Jenny flitted in to perch amidst the bramble thorns. 'I saw you bolt into this bush, so don't try to avoid capture and bolt out the back way. I'm sorry, but that's my job as a spy. Like me or loathe me, I just do what I'm told by whichever master I choose to serve. And at the moment it happens to be Nettles whom I love dearly. So don't try to make a dash for it, for I'll only track you down again. My advice is to give up your gold or face the terrible rage of Ruff. Unless you have a potent spell to ward him off – though I doubt it!'

'I beg you to surrender your gold for the sake of our valley, Berrybottom,' pleaded Sage. 'And for Finn and Pansy, your wounded comrades!'

'And me!' cried terrified Ossie. 'Deserting a ship is a capital crime in the eyes of Ollie . . . I mean Captain Ruff!'

'Perhaps I just *might* have a little gold tucked away,' said Berrybottom, reluctantly. 'Which I was saving for a rainy day . . .'

'Then admit it to Ruff, for here he comes!' cried excited Jenny. 'With a firm tread and an even firmer resolve, I'll wager!'

The sound of marching sea boots stopped suddenly outside the bramble hide. Then a voice roared out making everyone jump.

'Come out, you skulking swabs!' ordered Ruff. 'And these brambles are surrounded if that Berrybottom tries to nip out the back way.'

'I've already warned him against trying that dodge,' shouted gleeful Jenny.

Having no choice, the fugitives filed miserably out. First came Sage, the sharp look in her eye warning Ruff and his men not to take spiteful advantage of their triumph. Next came Pansy and Finn, the girl taking Finn's hobbling weight on her shoulder. Then came the wizard of The Briars, his eyes downcast, his grubby fingers clawing at his itchy skin. Last of all emerged Ossie, his childish face screwed up as if he were about to burst into tears. They lined up in a pathetic row before Ruff, who began to speak. His tone was rough, his message clear as he glared at Berrybottom.

'Gold is what we're interested in,' he said, harshly. '*You* have it and *we* want it. Though I swore a pact with Nettles to spare your lives, refuse to deliver and I'll order my men to burn and destroy this valley down to the last fried baby. What do you say, false wizard?'

Berrybottom looked at the anxious faces of his friends in hiding. Then with great dignity he stretched himself to his full height, his posture one of noble intent. For the grubby, scratching, wild-haired wizard of The Briars, this was quite a feat.

Though not a warrior and never a hero, he now looked both parts. Protectively he flung his arms around his friends and looked Ruff in the eye.

'My gold is yours, and I will lead you to it. But if this precious valley and its folk are harmed in any way, then I'll brew such a spell as to make you wish you'd stayed home in your icy northlands.'

'And another spell bites the dust,' giggled Jenny to herself. 'For like the rest of them, it'll never get off the ground!'

'I've already agreed to those terms,' snarled irritable Ruff. 'So where is your hidden gold?'

'A journey upstream, at my home in The Briars,' sighed Berrybottom. He looked up at the moonlit sky. 'But it is a dangerous trip if attempted at night, what with the rapids and snagging rocks and all.'

'In that case, we'll spend the night aboard our ship,' decided Ruff. 'Then we'll set off upstream at first light. You four from the brambles will be our hostages, in case the boy Nettles tries any tricks. As for that paw-wringing vole, she can go and potter in some sticky mud and mind her own business!'

'I'm not going back aboard that ship,' wept Ossie. 'I want to stay ashore with my sea boots on firm land!'

'Oh, I almost forgot our little deserter,' sneered Ruff. 'Enjoying your landlubber's life, are you? And what if you begin to pine for the roll of the deck under your feet? And have you thought about your grandma's grief if you don't return with us? Come back and join your crew mates, for they've missed you very much. And my cabin is in a terrible mess since you ran away from us!'

'Rejoin us and enjoy your share of the gold, Ossie,' urged his crew mates. 'We all promise never to use you for axe practice again.'

'Liars!' shouted Ossie. 'You know that Ollie will clap me in irons when we get back on board. Then when we reach deep water he'll throw me over the side for the crabs to gnaw at. You all know it's true because he's done it before!'

'If Ossie is thrown in irons, then you'll never see your gold,' said Berrybottom firmly. 'When you sail away he must be allowed to stay in the valley if he wishes. Do you agree to that, Captain Ruff?'

'Agreed,' snapped Ruff. '*Now* can we get going? These creepy green woods and all the hooting of those staring owls makes me nervous.'

'And the hairy things that rustle in the undergrowth,' shivered his crew. 'Let's get back to the sea, Captain Ruff. On that empty blueness without bushes, that's where we long to be!'

'Fall back in your column then,' bawled Ruff. 'And keep the hostages in the middle. And if we march into an ambush attack from Nettles, slaughter everyone without pity, all except for Berrybottom, who we need to make us all rich. Now, my sea dogs, march away and pray we fill our hold with gold this coming day . . .'

And so the sailors tramped out of the stifling woods and into the wide, starry night.

If the Willow clan high in their tree saw them

pass beneath they gave no sign. But then they hardly would; grievously beaten in battle they had wounds to lick, and plans to make.

Then Sage came bounding back to the oak. There were thankful cheers when she announced that, though badly wounded, Finn and Pansy still lived. And there were angry shouts when she reported that Ruff wasn't being true to his word about treating the fugitives well. In fact, they were now hostages, she said to outraged cries. And they would surely die if the invaders were denied the gold they craved. There was little sleep in the great oak that night, as the discussion dragged on and on – what to do, and how to do it? That was the question being thrashed out. At long last a firm plan was arrived at . . .

Fifteen

FROM MISERY TO HOPE

Once again Finn and Pansy found themselves inside a coil of rope on the deck of the ship. But this time their companion was Berrybottom. The pain from their injuries and the rank smelliness of their wizard friend made them cry out for fresh air and water. But the axe-wielding guard perched on top of the rope ignored their pleas. He was busy tapping his toes in time to the songs his drunken friends were singing.

Little Ossie was suffering too. He had been bound and hauled up the mast on a rope, and there he swung, his cries pitiful to hear as the crew took turns to singe the soles of his feet with hot lanterns. It was a cruel punishment for wishing to live his life ashore. A swift flogging would have been kinder. But Ruff had taken Ossie's desertion as a personal insult. Apart from the love of his grandma, Olaf Ruff had never known affection, he had never had a friend to turn to. Though admired for his fierceness, he had always been a loner, determined to make his mark upon the world. And now even Ossie, a mere lowly cabin-boy, had turned his back on him. For that he was making the poor boy pay. In fact, he was making the whole world pay for the misery of his life . . .

It was the end of another drunken night, the start of a hungover dawn. But the sun was rising golden bright, which was promising. An omen for a rewarding day, perhaps?

'Get up, you lazy swabs,' shouted Ruff, striding about, kicking his crew to their feet. 'This is to be our bonanza day. Ready the ship for the journey upstream! Get to your oars and be ready to pull when I give the word! And you, guard . . .'

'Aye, aye, Captain Ruff,' cried the crewman, jumping down from the coil of rope.

'Bring Berrybottom here,' Ruff ordered. 'He's to be our pilot on the journey upstream. Release the other two, but keep a close eye on them.'

'Aye, aye, Cap'n,' yelled the guard, springing into action.

'What about me, Ollie?' wailed a voice from above. It was Ossie, dizzily swinging at the end of his tether.

'Cut him down!' snapped Ruff. 'And give him ten lashes for daring to call me Ollie. He's been warned about that before.'

'Here's the wizard Berrybottom, Captain,' said a crewman, pushing his prisoner forward. 'I dipped his head in a barrel of water but he's still a bit groggy around the gills. Frankly, he doesn't seem the least bit magic to me.'

'I'll give him groggy,' said grim Ruff, hauling Berrybottom to the prow of the ship. 'I vow he'll feel even groggier when we've stripped him of his gold. So, phoney wizard, are you ready to guide us to your miserly hoard of wealth? Change your mind and I'll chop up your friends into little bits personally.'

'I'll do anything you say,' said miserable Berrybottom. 'Just please spare my friends!'

'Then row, my soon-to-be wealthy lads,' yelled Ruff to his crew. 'For there's gold galore at the end of the rainbow we seek!'

And so, after a few drunken miss-strokes, the ship nosed out into the currents of the stream. The rowers were further encouraged by Ruff's next words.

'Remember this day, my hearties,' he cried. 'As the day when we rowed upstream as poor sailors with an empty hold, and rowed back to become the richest sailors in the northlands!'

'I can't wait to fight off the pretty maidens who'll be desperate to marry me!' yelled a rower, missing a stroke in his excitement.

'*I* can't wait to see the pride on my grandma's face,' cried another.

'Nor the puzzlement on mine,' remarked his friend. 'She always said I'd amount to nothing, yet look at me now!'

'So row, lads, row,' urged Ruff, holding tight to Berrybottom's tunic. 'And I'll make sure that this slippery key to our future wealth doesn't escape.'

Quite unseen, a Willow Clan lookout stationed on a crag had been watching and listening closely. As soon as the ship had set sail, he cupped his hands and yelled up at the great oak, 'The ship has cast off from the shore, Nettles. And sails for The Briars of Berrybottom, I'll be bound!'

'Message received and understood,' came the faint reply from Nettles.

'Now you can come down from that crag and eat your breakfast stew,' shrilled the voice of Granny Willow. 'I can't keep warming it up for lookouts perched on rocks. Come down at once, and stop your nonsense!'

'Yes, Granny Willow,' yelled the hungry lookout. 'And warm me up a second helping!'

As the invaders' ship vanished around the first bend in the stream, another crew set sail. Sage had taken aboard her broad back a small party of Nettles, Poppy and two more, although Nettles was annoyed about the overcrowding.

'Nettles,' said Meadowsweet sensibly, 'if you wish to be remembered as a hero, then someone must write down the brave things you do. And I as clan historian *must* be on the spot to do it. Otherwise you'll remain a blank in the memories of the People.'

'As I've always been a blank in Meadowsweet's mind,' grinned Teasel. 'But I'm used to it now. One day she'll notice me and yell, "Wow!"'

'You can both come, but promise not to fidget,' frowned Poppy. 'We don't want Sage overturning in a crisis.'

With everything settled, Sage stroked away upstream in the wake of the invaders' ship. The party had visited The Briars before, so the vole slowed her pace as she neared the spot. They arrived to find the raiding ship riding at anchor at the place that led up to Berrybottom's home.

Drifting quietly up to the ship, Sage made fast to the hull with her paw. Then Nettles nimbly climbed the side to peer aboard. Ruff and his crew were gone. There were just three persons on the littered and smelly deck – the sorrowful figures of Finn and Pansy, and the axe-armed sailor who guarded them.

Nettles was deeply angered to see his friends in such a wounded and weakened state. Quietly he stole aboard and crept towards the guard. Too late the sailor saw him coming. He had barely raised his axe before Nettles had run him through with his sword. Then he was calling down to his comrades to come and help before any of the crew returned. Finn and Pansy were greatly relieved to be amongst friendly faces.

'Ruff and his men have gone to The Briars,' said urgent Finn. 'And they've taken Berrybottom with them to point out where he hides his gold. Please try to help him, for he was kind to us while we were in hiding.'

'And don't forget Ossie,' whispered Pansy. 'He also helped us and they've taken him too. The poor little soul has been dreadfully tortured by that wicked crew.'

'Poppy and I will do what we can,' soothed Nettles. He motioned to Meadowsweet and Teasel. Between them the four gently lowered Finn and Pansy down the side of the ship and on to Sage's waiting back.

'Dear friend,' hissed Nettles to Sage. 'Hurry them back to the oak. Then return as soon as possible. We four are going to find out what's going on at The Briars. If we need to make an urgent escape you'll be waiting, I pray.'

'I'll be waiting impatiently,' promised the loyal vole. 'Good luck to you all.' And she turned and swam back downstream, taking care to keep her injured cargo dry.

Nettles had never cared much for Berrybottom until now. But his opinion had changed. Any person who helped his family would be helped in return. Poppy, Meadowsweet and Teasel were in full agreement. Moments later they were swarming down the shore-side of the anchored ship. Soon they were hurrying along the path that led to The Briars and the shining pond of Berrybottom. The trail was muddied and well-trodden; it was clear that Ruff's men and their captives had recently passed along. As they neared The Briars the sound of loud voices and splashing could clearly be heard . . .

Sixteen

REFLECTIONS IN A POND

Ruff and his party had arrived some time before. Crabapple had been crouched over her fire, muttering into the flames. Hearing the sound of tramping feet she looked up, startled. But her surprise quickly turned to anger when she saw the private clearing filling up with rough-looking sailors with axes slung over their shoulders. She was not the least bit afraid, just absolutely furious.

'What do you want?' she screamed. 'If it's spells and potions you're after, that rascal Berrybottom is away collecting some gold we're owed.'

'Oh no he's not,' snapped Ruff. He dragged Berrybottom from amongst his escort and pushed him forward. The scruffy wizard looked cowed and very afraid as he stood before his wife. Crabapple looked scathingly at him. Then, noticing that his only possessions were his spell-pot and his ingredients pouch, her pinched face whitened with rage.

'Where's our three bags of gold?' she yelled. 'Didn't I warn you never to come back without it? And who's this rabble you've brought with you?'

'Actually, I didn't get the gold, dear,' interrupted nervous Berrybottom. 'In fact, these men are here to take our gold away . . .'

'What gold?' cried Crabapple, her eyes wide in alarm. 'There's no gold on this humble property. Didn't you tell them that, Berrybottom?'

'See how the morning sun reflects upon yon golden pond,' mocked Jenny from her perch. She eyed Crabapple with malicious glee. 'In fact, these large gentlemen have come to bathe in those inviting waters!'

'Oh no they're not,' yelled Crabapple, springing to her feet. She backed towards the pond, her arms held wide as if to protect it. 'Nobody ever bathes in these waters without paying with good gold. Take a running jump in the stream, for you're not jumping in here!'

'It's too late for lies, dear,' sighed her husband. 'I've promised to give Ruff and his raiders all the hoarded Berrybottom gold in return for peace in our valley.'

'Over my dead body!' cried Crabapple. 'Whatever gold Berrybottom has hoarded is to keep me in my old age. To steal it, you'll have to kill me first!'

'That can be arranged, old crone,' snarled Ruff, impatiently. Then he grabbed Berrybottom by his ragged tunic and glared into his eyes. 'Certain hints seem to tell me that the gold is hidden in your pond. Would I be right?'

'You are,' wheezed Berrybottom, near to choking. 'I was just about to tell you so.'

At his words the crew went wild with happiness. They broke ranks and made a mad dash for the glittering pond. Kneeling around the bank they whooped their delight to see their golden faces reflected back from the treasure lying heaped on the bottom. Soon they were diving in and returning to the surface clutching nuggets of gold and finely-wrought jewellery, all misered away by generations of Berrybottoms in payment for their phoney spells and potions.

While Berrybottom looked sadly on, Crabapple was throwing a fit. Her fury was such that her surge of alarming strength surprised Ruff and his men. She dashed to the pond, howling at the divers, her long nails scratching as she tried to snatch back their booty. Ruff harshly ordered her to be restrained and lashed to a tree. And there she writhed, screaming threats and vowing vengeance, all to no avail.

'Right, let's have some order, my rich Jack Tars,' bellowed Ruff. 'I want you to form a chain from this pool and down to the stream. That way we can pass the treasure from hand to hand, and load our hold more quickly.'

'Do you want me to stand in the chain too, Ollie?' asked Ossie, limping forward on his scorched feet. 'I'll do whatever you say, but please don't torture me any more.'

'Oh my, in the excitement I almost forgot about our little deserter,' mocked Ruff. Then roughly, 'Just get in the line, and I'll consider what to do with you when we're back at sea. And, for the *very* last time, *don't* call me Ollie!'

'No, Captain Ruff,' said the boy, shuffling away. 'I'll never call you Ollie again. You were never my friend. I know that now.'

And so began the shuttling of the wealth down to the ship. To the sound of raucous sea shanties a huge amount of glittering gold was packed into the hold. The crew didn't mind the sweaty toil at all, for now they were rich and would soon be basking in praise from families and grandmothers back home in the northlands. And they would be fighting off the pretty maidens who had once scoffed at them for being poor sailors.

Then a crewman came running back along the track to speak urgently to Ruff who was supervising at the pond. Fighting for breath, he gasped, 'Two things to tell you, my captain. First, the prisoners we left on board have escaped and our guard is dead. Second, the hold is full and our ship is lying dangerously low in the water.'

Ruff shrugged to hear that Finn and Pansy had escaped. He had got what he wanted, so they were no use to him anyway. Nor did he show regret or concern for a dead shipmate. But he was angry to hear that his ship could carry no more gold. He strode to the pond and gazed down into its depths. Shining temptingly on the bottom was still enough treasure to fill the holds of three more ships. His greed battled with his sea-sense. But his sea-sense won through. Better to return home with one holdful of gold, than to risk sinking because of an overload. Reluctantly, he ordered his chain of men to stop work.

'But there's still plenty left, Captain Ruff,' cried his men. 'Do you mean that we should leave it here? We've long dreamed about being rich, and now we are! But this is our chance to be mega-rich. We'll all become lords back in the northlands. We can all become cruel captains like you! We can each buy our own fleet of raiding ships if we empty this pond of gold. We don't mind the extra hard work, Captain Ruff!'

'Our ship won't bear any more weight,' snapped Ruff, as disappointed as them. 'But I promise you this, we *will* return. This valley has not seen the last of us. The next time we come we'll have a fleet of ships, to squeeze the last dreg of value from this pious, peaceful valley. And now back to the ship, for we need to make ready for our triumphant voyage home!'

And he hurried his men from the golden pond, snapping out instructions along the way. As callous as always he elbowed the owner of the pond aside. Berrybottom had served his purpose and that was the end of it – for the time being, of course. For Ruff was certain that the miserly wizard of The Briars would guard the rest of his gold, which would make him and his pond easy pickings when Ruff came back with more empty ships.

'So, guard your treasure well, stupid wizard,' he laughed at humbled Berrybottom. 'And keep it safe – for me!' And then he was gone . . .

Nettles and his party heard all this as they crouched in hiding at the edge of the clearing. They watched the hurried departure of the raiders with relief. But their eyes were drawn to a forlorn figure beside the pond, quite alone and ignored. It was Berrybottom. He was gazing at his trampled reeds, his muddy pond, the banks stamped with the prints of heavy sea boots. Scattered around were nuggets of gold and other discarded trinkets. He did not rage or weep as the watchers perhaps expected. Instead, he raised his head and forced a craggy-toothed grin. Then suddenly he flung his arms wide and began to speak his thoughts aloud. They were not the words of the miser he was known to be, but rather the words of someone who had seen a humbling light.

'What is gold but a bright possession?' he cried. 'Will it soothe an empty belly when hunger strikes? Will it keep you warm when you are cold? No, never. For though I was rich I lived a miserable and wretched life. I wronged my wives and cruelly spelled them to vanish, which they only halfway did. I couldn't even make a proper job of it, for the missing ingredient always eluded me. Now they wail in the bushes, trapped in a world of neither here nor there, the victims of my blundering. I can only apologize for the distress I've caused those ladies I accused of nagging me. Now I know that they were only doing it for my own good. I realize now that I *should* have bathed more often, told them I loved them every day, and not kicked their cooking in the air when it tasted vile. Yet the hoarded gold of the Berrybottoms has at least done some good. It has bought some precious time to plan against the next attack. Captain Ruff and his raiders have a holdful of gold to sail home to the northlands. Which means we are free from their evil presence in our valley for a while. Oh, the pride of this Berrybottom! That *I've* helped to stave off the total destruction of this wonderful valley. And the joy of this Berrybottom too! For now I have true friends for the first time in my life. Warm friends who have proved more precious than cold gold to this lonely sinner. My only grief is that little Ossie has been taken away from me. For he would have made a lovely little apprentice.'

The listening Nettles and his party were deeply moved by his words, and so were the three ghostly wives watching from their nether world behind the screening ferns. Then their voices were heard again, not taunting and hating this time, but gentled and almost forgiving.

'So you truly loved us, really,' sighed Nightshade.

'And deep down you loved us, dearly,' wept Leafmould.

'So you loved us all, quite clearly,' grieved Sourseed.

'In my old-fashioned way, sincerely!' cried Berrybottom, gazing at the white shapes flitting behind the bushes. 'It was just your constant nagging that made me lose my temper from time to time. Now will you stop persecuting me, and give me peace?'

His heartfelt plea was answered. At last the ghostly wives forgave him and could vanish from their half-world of torment into the peace of the heaven they craved. To the place where hatred turned to love, where nagging was forbidden.

Then Nettles and his friends emerged from their hide and approached the beaming born-again Berrybottom. Clustering around, they thanked him for sacrificing his gold for the sake of the valley. But there were no smiles from a certain person still tied to a tree. Crabapple began to kick and scream as she fought against her bonds, demanding to know why her good-for-nothing husband was being hailed as a hero, while *she* was still tied to a tree. Meadowsweet ran over quickly and freed the angry lady with a swift slice of her quill-cutting knife, which she kept in her sleeve.

'Now will you smile at last, Crabapple?' pleaded the girl. 'For now you can be proud of your husband! He's done something noble for the first time in his life. Isn't that wonderful?'

'*Wonderful?*' yelled Crabapple, pushing the girl aside. 'What's wonderful about having gold stolen from under your nose, while your cowardly husband does nothing?'

'But he did it to save the valley we share,' protested Meadowsweet. 'Surely a holdful of gold is worth the safety of us all?'

Meadowsweet was wasting her words. But Crabapple didn't waste any time, as she rushed at her husband and shoved him viciously into the pond. For a while Nettles feared for

Berrybottom's life, when all that broke the surface were bubbles and a host of fleas, desperately abandoning their homes in the wizard's filthy clothes.

'You craven coward,' cried Crabapple as Berrybottom's spluttering face appeared. 'How *dare* you allow foreign riff-raff to steal our treasure? How *dare* you take up good causes without my permission? *Why* should I care about these precious people and this hateful, happy valley? I married you to be seriously rich, not joyfully poor!'

'I've realized that gold isn't everything,' said Berrybottom, clambering out from his first bath in years. There was a dignity about him even as he stood dripping water and streams of ancient grime. 'But I don't expect you'll ever understand *that*, my poor embittered wife.'

'I know what I *do* understand,' cried Crabapple, boxing his ears. 'And you'd better understand it yourself, and quick! I demand that you replace every last scrap of stolen gold. So, what are you waiting for?'

'I'm waiting for you to stop nagging, dear,' said Berrybottom, patiently. 'And also for you to be more realistic. To replace all the stolen gold would take me the rest of my life.'

'If that's what it takes, then so be it!' spat Crabapple. 'And don't come back with more excuses and empty gold sacks! Now be off with you all. My fire is waiting to be gazed in, and I'm waiting to gaze in my fire . . .' and she turned on her heel and returned to crouch beside her flickering flames, cursing the valley and everyone in it.

'Come, let's get away,' urged Nettles. 'Sage will be waiting down at the stream. We must get back to the oak as quickly as possible. Who knows what vengeful things Ruff and his men might do if they arrive before us? Our duty is to be there to defend the family against any cruel trick that our enemies might play before departing.'

Sage was indeed waiting for them as they stumbled out of the muddy woods and down to the bank of the stream. To their surprise the invaders' ship still rode at anchor a short distance away, wallowing low in the water under her burden of gold. From the deck came the sounds of another drunken party in full swing. Ruff and his crew were celebrating their new status as rich sailors. Somewhere on board would be little Ossie, probably in chains, and no doubt trembling with fear as he waited for his fate to be decided by vicious Captain Ruff. But there was nothing the sad friends could do for him, however much they wished to.

Berrybottom was the most upset of all. He and Ossie had become close friends while hiding in the brambles, and now his small apprentice, a boy who could have been his son, was facing a grisly future quite alone. But this was not the time for sentiment. While the raiders' ship remained in the valley, no one was safe. Even as the party climbed aboard Sage's back for the journey home, they heard a plaintive cry drifting over the water from the ship. Everyone turned to see poor Ossie hanging from a rope over the side of the vessel, appealing for help and weeping for his grandma. Turning their backs on his plight was a wrenching thing to do. But the party had no choice as they set off downstream. Not a word was spoken during that journey. The grim expressions and tear-filled eyes were evidence enough of the feelings they all shared . . .

And then they were coasting into the shadow of the great oak that leaned across the waters like the arms of a welcoming parent. Jenny came winging in to perch on Sage's nose. As usual, she was full of chirpy gossip. But she held her tongue when she saw the suspicious look on Nettles' face. As the vole floated in to moor, allowing her passengers ashore, the boy-leader spoke.

'I'm beginning to wonder why you come and go so much, Jenny wren,' he said, eyeing her closely. 'We understand your comings, but not much about your goings. What do you get up to when you disappear so suddenly, so often? What game are you playing, secretive bird?'

'A spy never divulges her whereabouts,' was

the grinned reply. 'If I told you my secrets I'd be out of a job. Didn't you employ me to work undercover? If you sacked me I'd have to work for someone else. And that would break my heart, as your closest companion for life.'

'You were never his closest,' snapped jealous Poppy. 'I haven't once left Nettles' side since our troubles began!'

'Just do your job, Jenny,' said Nettles. 'So what have you got to tell us?'

'The ship has raised anchor and is rowing back this way. Bound for the sea, no doubt,' cried the bird. 'And I also bring you the dying words of poor Ossie. While dangling on the end of his torture rope, he gasped for Berrybottom to save him with a powerful spell. Then his body jerked and his eyes rolled up, to stare vacantly at nothing.'

'Ossie is dead?' raged Berrybottom. 'My very best friend and new apprentice? Someone will pay for this, when I get my spells back together. I adored that lad and meant to make him my

Berrybottom heir! Now my dreams are all shattered . . .' and he broke down in a flood of tears, that only a father could have shed. The friends rushed to comfort him.

But though Nettles sympathized, his thoughts were solely concerned with the welfare of the valley. Until Ruff's ship had departed the home of the People, the danger still remained. Would that vicious captain be content to sail away with his gold, or would he launch a parting attack out of sheer, malicious spite?

'Jenny,' he ordered, 'fly at once to Buttercup Hill and tell Umber and Amber to gather their warriors and meet me down at the beach. Quickly now!'

'Yes, my leader,' cried Jenny, flitting away.

'As for the rest of us, we'll proceed at once to the meeting hall,' said Nettles, 'where our anxious family waits for news of our triumph, or our fall . . .'

Seventeen

AN UGLY THREAT AND ONE SMALL TRIUMPH

The meeting hall that afternoon had never been so crowded. Everyone, young and old, had gathered to hear their fate, and that of their once-peaceful valley. The wounded warriors, including Finn and Pansy, had been laid on pallets at the front of the hall. As heroes it was proper that they should be close to the stage when Nettles honoured them for their bravery. And this was the first thing he did when he strode from the wings to address the assembly, Poppy and Berrybottom at his side. After murmuring some comforting words into the ears of the wounded and gently patting them on the head, he turned to the worried audience and began to speak.

'Dear family and friends,' he said, 'I'm relieved to tell you that the destruction of our valley has been averted for a while. Thanks to the change of heart and the generosity of Berrybottom, the invaders' lust for gold has been satisfied for now. But we don't know if their lust for blood has also been sated. As I speak, their ship is sailing back this way, with a holdful of gold from the pond at The Briars. The problem is that Berrybottom's pond still contains lots more treasure, which means that Ruff could return one day to steal the rest. But we'll have to face that worry when it comes. For the time being, all we wish is for the ship to leave our valley. Then, when it's back at sea, we'll have time to make plans to oppose the second invasion that Ruff might well launch in the near future.'

'Only we'll be twice as prepared for him the second time,' vowed Poppy. 'This valley will ring with the invaders' dying cries should their sea boots tread our land again!'

'And on and on the fighting will go,' sighed Sage. 'With never an end to it.'

'May I say something?' asked Berrybottom. He whispered into Nettles' ear that he wanted to make an important point about his personal life. Nettles agreed and turned the stage over to their hero wizard. Scratching himself as usual, Berrybottom blurted out his speech – a self-pitying and cunning one.

'I suppose you know that I gave away my gold to save this beautiful valley,' he said, wiping away a tear. 'But in doing so I lost the love of my beloved wife Crabapple. She's thrown me out of The Briars, my ancient home. Sadly I'm now single again, and very lonely. But don't feel sorry for me, all you lovely ladies! I'm sure I'll learn to live on my own for ever. I'm sure I'll learn to cook solitary meals with no one to enjoy them with.'

'Never!' cried the elderly ladies in the audience. 'You'll always be looked after by the Willow Clan. How could Crabapple treat you so cruelly? We've never heard of such an unmatched marriage. Stay, and make a new home with our Willow Clan, and you'll never be lonely again!'

Berrybottom beamed his craggy-toothed grin. In the meantime his sharp eyes had been scanning the adoring ladies for the one he hoped to make his next wife. He was looking for a perfect match, the lady least likely to be a nagger. His constant scratching had ceased. Despite his loss of gold he appeared to be a very contented and hopeful wizard. He was even considering regular baths, and fresh tunic changes.

'If we may return to our present, still dangerous, situation,' snapped Nettles. 'Time is passing, and Ruff's ship will soon be sailing past our oak on its way back to the sea. Let's hope that they don't delay in their eagerness to get back home, to be acclaimed as heroes and very rich sailors. Let's pray that they sail on by, for that's what I'd do in their place . . .'

'But we can't bank on it!' said Poppy fearfully. 'Ruff just might decide to wade ashore and wreak more havoc on our valley. And capture a few pretty maidens for marrying and gutting fish back in the north!'

'Which leads me to the crux of my speech,' shouted Nettles. 'I want every able-bodied person here to arm themselves with whatever weapons they can find. Then I want you all to rush down to the beach and prepare a last-ditch stand against the invaders, should they decide to come ashore again. Are you with me, my Willow People?'

'We are!' roared the audience, jumping up and milling around the door of the hall, each determined to be a hero, if just for one day.

Even Granny Willow had caught the mood. She snatched up her heaviest saucepan from the kitchen and hobbled after the rest on their rush down to the beach. She was determined to boff at least one invader on the head before she was dragged aboard the ship as a pretty maiden bound for the cold northlands. Rosie and Thorn, her kitchen-slaves, refused to be left behind. Wielding a large wooden spoon apiece they scampered after her. Their excitement knew no bounds. To become heroes after such a short time in the kitchen was a dream come true! No more chopping vegetables, no more scrubbing dirty dishes, they exalted. As they clambered down the trunk of the great oak, as they dashed towards the stream, it seemed that every step they took was one rung higher on the ladder to fame and fortune.

It was now late afternoon. It seemed that everyone in the valley was gathered on the beach as the spring sun cast setting shadows on the waters. Umber and Amber and most of their Guardian clan were there. Sage too, looking worried and sad as usual. Even Jenny was there, smirking at some secret thought, as she always was. And then the jostling and the babble of nervous voices died away. All eyes were turned to see the foaming bow and the heaving oars of the invaders' ship as it steered round the last bend in the stream and drifted in sluggish slowness towards the beach below the oak. Fearful, but bravely waiting, the rag-tag army of defenders gripped their makeshift weapons and held their breath. Then the heavily-laden vessel stopped in mid-stream on an order, the rowers fending the ship from the rocks with their oars. A harsh voice was clearly heard – that of Captain Olaf Ruff.

It was then that the fear of the defenders turned into pity and disgust. For, hanging from the side of the ship, was a rope. And tied to the end of that rope was the pathetic figure of Ossie, soaked and battered and crying for help. Such was the anger of the folk on shore that many had to be restrained from plunging into the water to rescue him. Strangely, Berrybottom just squatted on the sands and said nothing. He merely stared at the suffering Ossie, but did not react. Then Ruff appeared on the deck of his ship to sneer and threaten.

'A welcoming committee, eh?' he mocked. 'Or is it our going-away party? Well, don't bother, because we'll be coming back. The next time I come to this valley I'll be Admiral Olaf Ruff, with a fleet of ships under my command. Then, once I've emptied that pond of every last scrap of gold, I'll set about showing you how cruel I can really be. I'll lay waste to this happy valley of yours, for your contentment irritates me. I spit upon your loyalty and concern for one another, and the smugness of it all. Who do you think you are, to be so blessed? Perhaps you think that I've never known love?'

'Your granny always loved you, Ollie,' came Ossie's plaintive cry from the end of his tether. 'And she'd love you even more if you stopped torturing me and let me go back to my friends on the beach. She'll give you a dreadful scolding when she finds out what you did to me!'

'But she'll never find out,' crowed Ruff,

triumphantly. 'Because I intend to bury you at sea on a charge of mutiny. And none of my crew will breathe a word if they know what's good for them. I'll tell her that you died of seasickness, which is more or less the truth. Anyway, my granny believes everything I tell her.'

For the folk ashore, that was the final straw. Lying to a grandmother was the greatest crime of all. They were horrified.

But not so Berrybottom. Hearing Ruff's threat to bury Ossie at sea, he bellowed with rage. Throwing aside his spell-pot and shrugging off his ingredients pouch, he plunged into the stream. With clumsy but strong strokes he struck out for the ship, determined to rescue his best friend Ossie, or die in the attempt. Spurred on by the cheers from the shore, he ignored the axes that whistled down from the deck. Not even a thudding blow on his head caused him to miss a stroke as he swam grimly on. Seeing his plight, Nettles ordered his archers to fire a volley of arrows at the sailors bunched along the side of the ship. It had the desired effect as they hastily ducked their heads. Soon Berrybottom was spluttering and treading water beneath Ossie's swinging body. With strong fingers and toes he nimbly climbed the side of the ship and began to gnaw through the rope with his strong brown teeth. A few chomps of his jaws and the rope parted, sending Ossie splashing into the waters below. Berrybottom leapt down to join him. Then, grasping his small apprentice by the scruff of the neck, he struck back for the shore to howls of frustration from the deck, and to shouts of encouragement from the beach. Ruff was livid with anger. In fact, he was spitting mad with incandescent fury.

'Don't let that one small triumph go to your heads!' he raged. He brandished his axe and seemed about to jump over the side of the ship to take revenge. His men were in similar mood, and for a moment it seemed that they were about to storm ashore and attack the beach once more. But the heavily-laden hold of the ship put paid to that.

With all the rushing to and fro, the vessel lurched in protest on its side, its timbers creaking and groaning in warning. Seeing the danger, Ruff snapped out orders. Quickly the crew dashed across to the other side of the ship to even the balance. When the creaking and the groaning started there, they rushed to bunch at the centre of the deck. Their confusion was not lost on the folk who clustered the shore. Now it was their turn to taunt. They realized that Ruff and his men had a choice – they could wade ashore and crush the valley People once and for all, but that would risk overturning their ship and the precious gold it contained. On the other hand, they could stifle their urge to kill and wallow back to the northlands with their riches intact. Ruff made the wiser choice.

'Make everything shipshape, and prepare this vessel for sea,' he bellowed to his men. 'We'll settle our score with this rabble and their valley when we come back with a vast fleet of ships, all flying the banner of Admiral Olaf Ruff! But first we must get our riches safely home, there to bask in the hero-worship we so deserve, and the proud tears of those we love the most.'

'Which means our grandmothers,' cried his sailors, readying the ship for the final journey downstream where the wide blue sea awaited them.

'Ollie,' cried Ossie from the shore. 'Will you please give my love to my grandma when you get home? After all the punishment you've given to me, it's the least thing you can do.'

'You *dare* to ask a favour from me?' snarled Ruff. 'When I get home I intend to tell your dear grandma that you deserted your ship and sneered at her memory when I tried to change your mind. Her grey hair will turn white with grief when she hears what a cringing coward you turned out to be. And then her hair will all fall out when I tell her that you died a seasick failure!'

Ossie collapsed in tears. Shaking with anger Berrybottom put a comforting arm around him.

'Have you any more wicked things to say before

you sail away?' cried Nettles in disgust.

'Only this,' glowered Ruff, 'that you and your flower-sniffing friends should tremble night and day when we have gone. For I'll return when you least expect it, ten times as powerful and ten times as angry! So don't say you weren't warned . . .' and with those ominous words he ordered his oarsmen to bend to their task, rowing their ship back down to the mouth of the stream. Soon the wallowing ship with its cargo of gold was steering a lurching course through the rocks and rapids as dusk began to fall. The last sight was its deck lanterns, twinkling like fireflies in the fading light, and the last sounds were the lusty rowing songs of the now rich and jubilant crew.

Oh, what epic tales of adventure they would spin when back amongst their northern folk! How they yearned for the wide sea to be crossed as quickly as possible! How they ached to swagger and spill golden trinkets into the palms of their cringing admirers! How wonderful it would be to snub those who had scorned them as vagabond sailors, thinking they would never amount to anything! But most of all the crew of the ship desired the approval of their grandmothers, as did their fierce captain. Those adored old ladies who had nursed and nurtured them, who had thrilled and frightened them with stories of monsters who howled and scratched outside their icy cabin doors. Those wrinkled ladies who had soothed them with tales of ancient northern heroes, whose warm arms had snuggled them tight through the long winter nights that never seemed to end. Now, at last, the invaders could see an end to their quest to prove themselves, and they had lots of bright gold to prove their worth. Not only that, but there was plenty more where their holdful had come from. No wonder they sang their rowing songs more heartily than ever as they left the valley far behind. For the world was now their oyster, and a golden one at that . . .

Eighteen

OSSIE'S MAGIC MOMENT

There was great relief amongst the People of the valley as their enemies departed. It was suggested by some that the event should be celebrated with a party right there on the beach. But wiser minds urged caution. Though peace *had* returned, it was surely just a lull before the next storm, and they had no doubt that Ruff and his men would return, in greater force. The huge bulk of gold still glittering beneath the waters of Berrybottom's pond ensured that. Before they left the beach Nettles had some words to say.

'We cannot undo what is done,' he lamented. 'Our valley has been discovered, and there's nothing we can do to change that. We must accept that Ruff and his men will return, for the lure of gold will certainly bring them back. So we must plan for the dark days ahead. We must make the defences of our valley strong enough to throw back their next attack.'

'Perhaps Ruff's ship will sink while crossing the sea,' offered hopeful Umber. 'Perhaps the weight of all that gold will drag them down to a watery grave.'

'Leaving no trace behind,' nodded Amber. 'If Ruff and his ship never arrive home then the people of the northlands would never know about our valley and about Berrybottom's treasure pond.'

'Only the fishes would ever know,' said

Meadowsweet, wisely. 'I've studied fishes for a long underwater poem I'm writing. And they'll say nothing at all, for though they open and close their mouths a lot, no words ever pass their lips. So the secret would be safe with them. I've listened for ages with my head underwater, and all I've ever heard from the fishes were gulps and burps. Luckily I didn't drown during my research.'

'Because I was holding her feet,' grinned Teasel. 'To allow a poet of her genius to drown would be a terrible crime!'

'We can't rely on Ruff's ship sinking,' said Nettles, impatiently. 'What we need is some strong defence that will deter all future invaders.'

'Like a miracle,' said Poppy, wistfully.

'If I could say a word,' interrupted Ossie, shyly. 'My master and friend, Berrybottom of The Briars, is wonderful at miracles. As his new apprentice I'm totally in awe of his skills.'

'Berrybottom might have had a change of heart, but he's still a phoney wizard,' snapped Jenny.

'We all know that his spells never work, apart from causing his ex-wives to run around in the woods, dressed up as ghosts and cackling silly curses.'

'Yet his potions and spells cured the wounds of Finn and Pansy in the bramble bush,' insisted loyal Ossie. 'Perhaps if we encouraged him he could produce the miracle we desperately need.'

'What do you say, Berrybottom?' questioned hopeful Nettles. 'Could you produce just one successful spell from all your failures? If you tried extra hard, could you save our valley with some more of your mumbo-jumbo?'

'Just give me one chance to prove myself,' begged Berrybottom. 'I need just one more ingredient to complete the vanishing spell my forefathers failed to find. And I'm sure it's near to hand, so near that I feel I can almost smell it.'

In fact, the missing ingredient was definitely near to hand. Indeed, not much more than a good sniff away. But no one knew that as yet.

'I've got a feeling that I'll find it at the top of

Buttercup Hill,' he said, mysteriously. 'And spells usually work best on the tops of hills. Especially miracle ones.'

'Well, there's only one miracle I'm interested in,' snorted Granny Willow. 'And that is the hope that my new trainee-cooks have had the good sense to take my hot pans off the fierce heat while I've been protecting our land.'

'We can't be in two places at once, Granny Willow,' protested Rosie and Thorn. They were standing behind her, wooden spoons tucked into their belts like swords. 'We can't defend our valley *and* juggle your hot pots and pans at the same time!'

'What are you two doing here?' cried the angry lady. 'How dare you leave my kitchen unattended and without my permission?'

'You left it as well, Granny Willow,' replied the defiant pair. They were about to say more, but they were stopped short. Grasping both of them by their ears the old lady hurried them back to their place of work. Their 'ouches' and squirming didn't touch Granny Willow's usually soft heart one bit.

The night was clear and starry as Nettles and Umber led their followers from the bank of the stream. Some Willow Clan members dropped out when they reached the great oak as they had important business to attend to. The rest of the party then moved on to begin the steep, wearying climb up Buttercup Hill. They had little faith in the powers of Berrybottom. But they had total faith in Nettles and Umber, their leaders. Surely *they* knew what they were doing, even if no one else did?

Yet Nettles and Umber looked very subdued as they led the way to where the camp-fires blazed at the top, where the Guardian folk crouched around the flames that lit up the giant, snoozing head of their Great Golden Snake. From children to adults, all looked fearful and anxious when Umber tried to calm their nerves. Especially when they saw Berrybottom, who had scoffed most of their fish suppers and had stolen the golden dandruff of their great snake on his last visit. For that scruffy wizard seemed to rhyme with bad news.

'My People of the Guardian Clan,' cried Umber. 'Quite soon we're going to witness a miracle performed by the great wizard, Berrybottom of The Briars. A miracle that will save our valley and our way of life from the invaders who came and shed our blood so cruelly. We all agree that Berrybottom doesn't look very magical. But we must all try to believe he is. For believing otherwise could destroy every belief in all things worth believing in.'

'Is it the same as believing in our Great Golden Snake?' piped a young voice from a fireside. 'You forced us to believe in him. For myself, I'm tired of dragging heavy stones to build Snakehenge. And he never thanks us, he just snores. Is that the kind of belief you're talking about? A belief always ordered by you grown-ups?'

'Exactly that,' said Amber, firmly. 'So I want all you little ones to cross your fingers and your toes when the wizard Berrybottom performs the tricks of his trade. And there will be no sniggering if he does silly things from time to time. Wizards are supposed to act strangely while conjuring spells.'

'We'll be as solemn as owls,' promised the youngsters, stifling their sniggers. 'But if Berrybottom starts to scratch his armpits and other personal places then we'll have to laugh out loud. For he's very funny when he's itchy.'

'Be quiet, and be still,' ordered Amber. 'Nettles of the Willow Clan is about to make an announcement.'

'People of the valley,' cried Nettles, striding forward. 'Guardians of the Great Golden Snake, lend me your ears. Berrybottom is here to help us, not to amuse us. So please raise a hearty cheer for the wizard who's promised to save our valley from the threat of invasion, for ever!'

'Get ready for the miracle,' cried the youngsters, cheering wildly. 'For here comes the great wizard, Berrybottom of The Briars!'

Then Berrybottom came shambling into the

light of the flickering fires, his spell-pot in his hand. He didn't look very confident as he gazed around at the host of trusting faces. He tried to grin, but it was a forced attempt. Close at his side was Ossie, his best friend and apprentice. The former cabin-boy had no doubts about his master's powers. Then a cry rose up from the Guardians.

'Look,' they shouted, pointing. 'Our great snake is weeping in his sleep. Perhaps he senses in his dream that the valley is in danger, and he's grieving for us. Perhaps he knows that Berrybottom is our only hope, and he's not impressed!'

Stung by those words Berrybottom sprang into action. Hurrying across to the nose of the great snake he caught a huge plopping tear in his spell-pot. Then he approached the nearest fire and settled his pot amongst the hot embers. Shrugging off his ingredients pouch he emptied its whole disagreeable contents into his brew. Then he stood back and waited for it to simmer. Save for the spitting and crackling of fires, the hill was hushed as everyone waited with bated breath for Berrybottom's miracle to begin. But not Jenny. She was hopping impatiently on her twig.

'I'm not standing around to watch Berrybottom make a fool of himself again,' she complained. 'I've still got some spying to do. Ruff and his ship should be leaving the valley quite soon, if they're still afloat with all that gold they're carrying. I'll just go and check, Nettles my leader.'

'Do what you think is best,' murmured Nettles, absently. 'And fly away quietly. We're trying to watch a miracle.'

'Goodbye then, my close companion for life,' smiled Jenny. 'I'll see you in the morning light, just when the night is through. Come the miracles in life, I'll still be seeing you . . .' and on tiny wings she sped away with cunning in her heart, and treachery too. For she hated things that turned out well and happily ever after. For where was the thrill in that? In truth she was a wicked little bird, if Nettles only knew. But quite soon her deceit would catch up with her, to destroy her tiny world . . .

Meanwhile, everyone's attention was on the unkempt figure of Berrybottom, who was fluttering his hands and muttering strange words over his bubbling spell. Many of the watchers were spellbound – they were actually watching a wizard in the process of weaving his powerful magic! In fact, what they were seeing was a failed wizard praying that from somewhere the vital ingredient he needed to complete his spell would appear to save his face, but more important, to save the valley. His frustration knew no bounds. He was still certain that the vital ingredient was no more than a sniffing pace away – but where could it be? Raising his hands up to the sky and throwing back his head he yelled an appeal to the cold, glittering stars . . .

'All our hopes are in this brew,
So I cry this plea to you,
Please reveal the vital clue,
And let our valley live . . .'

For long moments the stars shone down unheedingly. Perhaps the desperate appeal from a failed wizard was of no account in the vastness of the universe. Then, suddenly a shooting star came arching from the sky. Briefly it bathed little Ossie in its brilliant light before plunging to bury itself in the black earth on the hill.

Then, as if in a dream, Ossie slipped his hand inside his tunic and pulled out the plant that had caught his fancy as he and his friends had cowered in their bramble hide. Holding it high he stared at it without understanding. By his side Berrybottom was also looking bewildered and puzzled. Was his new apprentice trying to steal the show? And then a look of dawning came over the craggy face of the wizard of The Briars. All at once he knew. Nettles and Poppy were also staring; though they had no clue to its meaning, they identified the plant immediately.

'It's the plant of the tiny red flower that hides amongst the brambles,' whispered Nettles to Poppy. 'Remember when Granny Willow sent us down to the stream to pick a sprig, to make her stews taste heavenly?'

'Her secret ingredient!' gasped Poppy. Then she grasped his arm. 'But just look at the root of the secret flower, Nettles!'

By this time everyone on Buttercup Hill had noticed and was staring in awe. The root of the red flower was glowing a wonderful, luminous blue and was pulsating in time with the thumping of their own hearts. Then, still in his dream-like state, Ossie dropped the plant into Berrybottom's spell-pot . . .

And from that moment the People of the valley knew that things would never be the same again. The earth on which they stood gave a violent lurch, and the stars in the heavens spun around in dizzy circles before settling into a brand-new kaleidoscope of order in the sky. Immediately the earth became steady and firm once more, and the stars shone in their changed patterns as if they always had. All this had happened in mere moments, and now everything seemed to be normal again. But the People of the valley knew they had witnessed a miracle. Whether it would save their valley, and their way of life, they could not know just yet. But one thing was certain. Things would never be the same again . . .

Nineteen

ONCE THERE WAS A VALLEY

Jenny was perched on the side of Ruff's ship as it wallowed from the stream and out into the open sea. For a while she was content to watch the sweating rowers leaning to their oars while Ruff moved amongst them, cracking his whip and urging them on to greater efforts. Then her teasing, taunting self took over.

'Ahoy there,' she shrilled. 'Brace your binnacles and hoist your barnacles for a safe journey home, my lucky lads. Avast there, Captain Ruff. Splice the mainbrace, and crack open a barrel of ale for those thirsty sailors!'

'Why your sudden interest in our welfare?' snarled Ruff. 'Why should you wish us a safe journey home? Aren't you supposed to be the faithful spy of Nettles?'

'Sometimes, but not always,' smiled Jenny. 'Most times I'm my own bird and always will be. I do what I wish when I want. I say what I want when I wish. And what I say and wish and want usually gets granted by some means or other.'

'So what do you want from us, small turncoat bird?' asked curious Ruff.

'I want you to get safely back to the northlands,' giggled Jenny, her black eyes glittering. 'And then with your stolen riches, I want you to build a great fleet of ships and return to the valley of the People. I don't need to tell you that the whole of their valley is yours to exploit.'

'Then why tell me something I already know?' snapped Ruff. 'I don't need a treacherous wren to tell me *that*.'

'But I could help you when you return,' insisted Jenny. 'I could whisper in your ear about the defences they're building against your second attack. I could pretend to be the close companion of Nettles, while really being *your* obedient bird.'

'Treachery at its very best,' smiled Ruff, grimly. 'And what do you get from all this? What is it you want so much, Jenny wren?'

'Delicious excitement,' came the gleeful reply. 'The thrill of always being on the spot when epic things are happening. For I intend to die in happiness, not in boredom. Why should I care if some trusting souls are hurt along the way?'

'Spoken after my own heart,' chuckled Captain Olaf Ruff. 'We have a deal, my feathered traitor.'

'So, good sailing then,' cried Jenny, taking off and wheeling back towards the valley. 'And I hope to see you sooner rather than later . . .'

Glorying in her devilment Jenny flew back to

the mouth of the stream, and following its familiar course she began to wing her way happily home. Then, to her bewilderment, she found herself completely lost. She began to dart this way and that, but try as she might she could not get her bearings. The stream she knew so well had vanished at a point just above the rapids where she had first sighted the bristling ship. The valley so long her home was no longer there. In its place was just a desert shrouded in a blanket of cold mist. After a few more fluttering attempts to locate the elusive land, panic set in. Tired and confused she settled on a twig to pass away the night, her reeling head tucked under her wing for comfort. With the rising of the sun she flew down to splash herself awake in a small pool of water. Then, shaking her head to rid it of the nightmare, she gave herself a good scolding.

'Stupid bird,' she snapped. 'Pull yourself together. You should know your way home with your eyes shut! What kind of spy are you who blunders like an idiot in the dark?'

Once more she launched herself into the air and sped to the head of the rapids, only to become as lost as she had before. She returned bewildered to the twig and tried to reason things out. Something must have happened while she had been away, but what? Her thoughts went back to the previous evening on Buttercup Hill, when she had sneered at Berrybottom's attempt to perform a miracle that would save the valley and its People. Oh, surely not, she moaned inside. Had the vanishing spell succeeded after all? Yet it must have done, for where was the valley, her home? After lots more thought and many more tears the awful truth sank in. Lonely and desperately afraid she soared into the sky and began to batter her wings against the unseen force that barred her from the world she loved to bustle and spy in, now denied to her . . .

'Please let me in,' she wailed. 'I want to come home. I'll die outside here all alone. Nettles, my closest companion for life, forgive me my sins and allow a little bird to return and make amends . . .'

But the hidden valley kept its silence and its presence from the world outside. A miracle had indeed happened, but a miracle with a twist. The spell of Berrybottom and Ossie's vital ingredient had not vanished the enemies of the valley, but had vanished the valley itself. Lost outside for ever, mourned poor Jenny wren, as she sobbed and grieved and waited in hopeless hope for the mercy she knew she would never find . . .

A year passed and spring came round again. For the northerners it was the start of their new raiding and plundering season.

'But I'm certain that this is the right stream,' snapped Admiral Ruff, puzzling and poring over his map. He stabbed down a finger. 'See, I marked it clearly. Then just beyond this point are the rapids. Then a day's row up the stream we'll come to the valley of the People, then further up around the bend, we'll arrive at the pool where the wizard Berrybottom hoards his gold.'

'Yet this stream seems to lead to nowhere, sir,'

said his first officer, shaking his head. 'Three times we've rowed our ship to this point, and three times the stream has petered out as if it didn't exist. And all the rowers in your fleet are tired and becoming mutinous, sir. If you listen you can hear them breaking open the barrels of ale with their axes. With respect, Admiral Ruff, there's no water passage to sail beyond this point. Give us water to sail and we'll sail it, sir. But without waves to tackle how can we be sailors?'

'But that valley is up this stream somewhere!' bellowed frustrated Ruff. 'A green valley flowing with milk and honey and with lots of pretty maidens to carry home as brides. You do believe me, don't you?'

'Of course, sir,' said the nervous officer. 'I'm just saying that our ships are having trouble finding it.'

'You just wait till you see the golden pond of Berrybottom,' roared Ruff, a mad light in his eyes. 'I tell you, there's enough gold in those waters to fill every hold in this fleet, and more! So come on, try again. I'm ordering you to row up this stream that I've marked on my map, for I've got an old score to settle with a certain Nettles who lives in that valley. And not forgetting a turncoat cabin-boy who deserted his ship when the going got tough. I tell you, I'm determined to find that valley no matter how long it takes!'

'Perhaps we've got the wrong stream, sir,' suggested the officer, glancing meaningfully at his friends who fidgeted behind him. 'Perhaps you're over-tired, Admiral. Perhaps you'd like a nice lie-down . . .' and with that, they pounced on Olaf Ruff and bound him fast with rope. Ignoring his threats and curses they carried him below deck and shackled him to his bunk. In fact the very same bunk that a little cabin-boy called Ossie had kept so tidy in the sailing days gone by.

'Let me go, you scurvy swabs!' raged Ruff. 'I'll see every one of you fed to the crabs when I get free. I'm not mad, I tell you! I'm certain that there's a valley just up that stream, waiting to be ravaged and plundered. Go and check, it's all marked down on the map I drew when I was last here! Are there no members of my old crew to bear me out?'

'They're all living rich and successful lives back home in the north, we believe,' said the first officer. 'And looking after their grandmothers as you failed to do.'

'But I need to make her even more proud of me,' sobbed Ruff. 'That's why I built this fleet of ships and came back for the rest of Berrybottom's gold! Once there *was* a valley, I just know it . . .'

'In your dreams, but not in ours, sir,' murmured his officers, turning the fleet for home and sanity . . .

Indeed, there once was a beautiful valley, a place where the People had lived for countless generations. And a stream ran past it. And on the bank of the flowing stream grew a great oak tree, the home of the folk of the Willow Clan. Above the oak there was a hill, sun-bright with buttercups. And ringed around the valley was a

Great Golden Snake who was fast asleep, who would dream for one hundred years . . .

Still there is a valley. And the People weep and laugh and welcome the seasons as people everywhere. But now it is a hidden valley, lost somewhere in time and space, and ever more will it be so . . .

Dream on, my People, for a bright new day is dawning . . .